D0211548

The Secret Letter

Mary Blount Christian

CountrySamplerFiction.com

Library of Congress-in-Publication Data
The Secret Letter / by Mary Blount Christian
p. cm.
I. Title
                    2015921342

CountrySamplerFiction.com
(800) 282-6643
Antique Shop Mysteries™
Series Creator: Shari Lohner
Series Editor: Shari Lohner
Cover Illustrator: Bonnie Lieck

10 11 12 13 14 | Printed in China | 9 8 7 6 5 4 3

"Love is much like a wild rose, beautiful and calm, but willing to draw blood in its defense."

—Mark Overby

1

Maggie Watson leaned against the doorframe of her favorite guest bedroom in Sedgwick Manor, reminiscing about her daughter's childhood and time they had spent in this cozy room. The warm yellow on the original plaster walls was cheery and bright, lit by the sun rising over the ocean. The wispy sheer curtains, crewel-embroidered quilt, and humpback trunk at the foot of the bed were exactly as she remembered them from at least fifteen years before.

As the recent heir of her late Aunt Evelyn's nineteenth-century Colonial Revival house, Maggie wanted to add a few personal touches to make it feel like her own. She thought this beautiful room would be nice for her daughter, Emily, when she visited.

It had been only the two of them after her husband, Richard, died suddenly three years before. Now, with Emily an hour away, studying to be a nurse at St. Joseph's College, Maggie felt ready to begin a new phase in her life as she adjusted to an empty nest.

Still, she had celebrated a little the other morning when she flipped her calendar to November and started the countdown until she would see her daughter. It was going to be their first Thanksgiving in this lovely old manor, and she wanted to make it perfect for Emily.

At the sound of a creak overhead, Maggie recoiled. A flock of goose bumps raced up her arms, and she tightly pulled her chenille robe around her.

"Settle down," she said aloud. "It's nothing."

Yet she had the creepy feeling that she wasn't alone, thanks to those phantom footsteps and the eerie way her cat, Snickers, stared into empty spaces. *Enough!* It was a big old house. Naturally it would react loudly to the rapidly cooling temperatures typical of fall in Maine. As for Snickers's behavior, that was simply her cat being a cat.

She frowned at the cacti prints on the wall. Aunt Evelyn must have added them after Maggie's last visit. She jotted in her notepad, *Replace botanical art.* A few cross-stitched nautical samplers would fit better with the rocky Maine coastline beyond the sheer curtains.

Maggie was fond of making lists—groceries, projects, chores. They had always helped her stay organized but were particularly useful after she became a widow. Now, with an estate to run and a whole new set of responsibilities, she was relying more and more on her notepad.

Something brushed her leg, and Maggie startled. She sighed in relief as her tabby cat leaped onto the bed.

"I haven't forgotten you, Snickers. You're at the top of the list. See? It says 'Pet the cat' right here."

She scratched him behind the ears, and he broke into a rumbling purr. Maggie scooped up Snickers and walked to the window of the room she was now thinking of as Emily's. The sun was above the horizon, and the seagulls had taken to the air, circling and diving.

Some days she had to pinch herself to see if it was really true that she now owned this grand estate in the quaint town of Somerset Harbor. It was a dream come true, as was owning the Carriage House Antiques shop, just a short walk away on the estate grounds, where she could pursue her interest in antiquing.

But what about her little cottage in Bennington, Vermont, where she had lived nearly all of her adult life? What would Emily think if Maggie permanently moved to Sedgwick Manor and abandoned their home?

Snickers jumped from her arms to the floor and rubbed against the humpback trunk. Its colorful vaudeville stickers were nearly pristine. The gash where a younger Emily had hit it with her toy was still visible. Maggie ran her finger along the deep cut. She'd been horrified when it happened. But Aunt Evelyn had merely shrugged and said, "Nonsense. This was made to be used and abused. We can cherish antiques and admire them, but we owe them no more consideration than their original owners gave."

She flipped the latch and opened the lid. It smelled clean, like fresh linens. She wondered how her aunt managed to keep such an old piece from getting musty, especially living by the sea. Maggie pulled out a hand-stitched quilt and unfolded it. It featured a pattern of New England lighthouses. She'd put it on the bed. Emily would like it.

She noticed that the lining in the trunk had deteriorated in places. Many old trunks had paper linings, but the lovely material Maggie was looking at meant that the piece had been custom-made and expensive. Replacing the fabric and refinishing the gash could be her first project toward putting her own imprint on her new home.

Maggie added to her list, *Repair trunk*.

She closed the lid, returned to the window, and pulled the curtain aside. For a moment she imagined Emily as a little girl standing there with her, peering at the flying gulls. But Emily was officially an adult now, a woman in her own right who was living her life out from under her mother's wing. She swallowed hard and dropped the sheer curtain back into place. Her daughter had grown up so fast; Maggie wasn't sure she'd adjusted to it yet.

As she turned back to the room, she had the urge to knock on the walls in search of the hidden tunnels that supposedly existed inside Sedgwick Manor but that she'd never found. Unable to contain her curiosity, she pulled the bedside table away from the wall, nearly tipping over the hurricane lamp. It was identical to one Aunt Evelyn had given her. *Why would she have broken up the set?*

People who didn't know Evelyn Bradbury might have thought she acted erratically, but Maggie knew that wasn't the case. Everything Aunt Evelyn did was done with purpose, including writing cryptic notes she had left behind without explanation. It was up to others to figure out what she meant.

She and her aunt had shared many a delightful phone conversation about the mystery novels they both enjoyed. Perhaps her aunt had believed that Maggie would be up to the task of unraveling the mysteries she'd left behind in her journal.

Maggie ran her fingertips lightly over the textured iris blooms on the lamp's ruby glass globe. The lower half of the lamp featured cherub faces sitting on a brass base with four lion paws. Instead of felt padding, paper was glued to the bottom. *Odd.* Maggie made another note: *Replace vellum on lamp.*

Back downstairs, Maggie passed the library where the old portrait of Captain Thomas Sedgwick caught her eye. He was a naval officer who had built Sedgwick Manor for his wife, Abigail, with his inherited fortune. The captain's suspicious eyes seemed to follow her with disapproval.

Maggie stopped and leveled a look at the former owner. "Get used to us or you're getting donated to the historical society."

In her own room, she dressed for the day in her tan ottoman-stitch sweater and favorite jeans that fit comfortably over her brown leather boots. She gave her highlighted hair a critical look in the mirror and raked her fingers through the casual waves that fell above her shoulders. "Good enough. Who are you trying to impress?"

She retrieved her green windbreaker and stepped outside. The salty, gusting wind off the ocean had increased and the whitecaps rolled in, colliding with the rocks to send spray shooting into the air like geysers. She zipped her jacket and pulled the hood over her ears.

Maggie made The Busy Bean a regular stop on her daily walk. The coffee shop had become something of a refuge from the empty manor. The company was pleasant, and the brew gave her comfort on these chilly mornings.

As she entered the café, the bell above the door jingled and heads turned. Maggie was still getting to know everyone in town, but the locals already greeted her as an old friend.

"Storm's coming," said Daisy Carter, the coffee shop's owner, in her southern drawl. Tall and slender, today she wore her long, thick, brunet hair in a French twist secured with silver combs—a style that was more conservative than her usual hairdos. Her sapphire eyes were bright and sparkly beneath a generous slather of silvery-blue shadow.

At fifty-eight, Daisy exuded an absolute joy for life. It was easy to understand how she had earned the title of Miss Savannah in her youth. The Georgia native had moved to Somerset Harbor when she won The Busy Bean in an essay contest held by the previous owner. Her heart had been won in return by local fisherman Harry Carter, and she was now a staple of the community.

Daisy poured a mug of coffee from the pot and slid it forward across the counter. "When are you going to try one of my special blends?"

"Soon," Maggie promised. "What makes you think a storm is coming? It's windy, but the sun's out."

"I can smell it in the air." She threw her head back and gave a dramatic sniff. "Besides, I heard it on the weather station."

Maggie laughed. She should have known. Talk of the weather in Somerset Harbor wasn't simply "making conversation." Most had family in the lobster trade, so it was their business to know which way the winds blew.

"I wish Harry would head back to shore. I'll never get used to him being out there, bouncing around on the water like that."

Although Maggie had yet to meet Harry Carter, it was clear that Daisy was still deeply in love with him. The years seemed to fade from her face when she mentioned his name.

"We have a couple of hours before it hits, though," Daisy continued as she busied herself behind the counter. "You have plenty of time for a blueberry scone."

Maggie agreed, and Daisy plucked it from the display case and popped it into the warmer. "How's it going at the manor?"

"Not bad. I'm getting used to the night sounds . . . sort of. Does the wind ever stop?"

"Sure, it slows to a nice breeze in the summer." Daisy looked up as the bell over the entrance jingled. "I think someone's coming your way."

James Bennett—in gray-blue running gear that brought out the intense color of his eyes—shook hands with a few of the patrons and nodded to others. He paused to talk about replacing street signs and getting trees trimmed away from electrical lines. As an alderman and historic preservationist, he took care of Somerset Harbor.

"I'll have the usual," he told Daisy, and then he turned to Maggie. "May I join you?"

"Sure. Why don't we move over to the table by the window?" She enjoyed his company and already considered him a friend. He was her age, forty-four, and single, as everyone she met in the town mentioned—frequently.

Although she'd come a long way in dealing with Richard's death, she still carried the loss with her like an overstuffed suitcase. Only recently had she found the weight easier to manage. But she wasn't looking for romance—just friends whose company she enjoyed.

"Daisy, you're looking lovely," James said.

"I always look good with apple pie in my hand." Daisy set down his coffee and pie.

He immediately picked up his fork and took a bite.

"It's excellent." He beamed at Daisy. "As always."

Maggie shook her head in amusement. *No wonder he continues to be elected alderman.*

With her warm scone in hand, they settled at a table. "I need a professional consultation." Maggie looked down at her watch. "I'll start the clock now."

"I waive my fee when there's coffee and pie. How can I help?"

"I think I have the skills to refurbish an antique trunk myself. It has one semi-deep scratch and a few superficial ones, but it needs to be completely relined. I'd like to keep the new lining similar to the original fabric, but I have no idea if that's doable."

"It's definitely possible," James said with a nod. "I can show you some swatches. It doesn't take more than a day or two for delivery." He greeted a man who passed their table. "Harrison, good to see you." Returning his gaze to Maggie, he asked, "Does this mean you're officially making Somerset Harbor your permanent home?"

"I've gotten as far as thinking I might stay here for Thanksgiving," Maggie said. "It'll be easier for Emily to get to the manor than to Bennington."

"So, you're possibly committing to staying a few weeks," James teased. "I guess we'll take what we can get."

Maggie gestured at the darkening sky. "I want to see what kind of winters Maine has before I consider living here full time. It's getting ugly out there. Looks like a big one."

"Nah, it'll only be a squall. If you'd like, I can take a peek at that trunk now while I'm thinking about it. Later, I have some work to do in a Colonial a few miles up the coast."

Grateful for the help, Maggie agreed, and they enjoyed their coffee over talk of the historic preservation work James had in store for the rest of his day.

"My treat," she said, ignoring James's protests and placing cash on the table when they were finished.

As they prepared to leave, Maggie noticed that most of the lobster boats were heading for shore. The water churned, looking like cappuccino with frothy whitecaps. *Only a squall?*

She zipped her windbreaker and left The Busy Bean with James at her side.

· · · · · · · · · · · · · · · · ·

Back at Sedgwick Manor, Maggie stooped to hold Snickers securely until James was inside and the door was shut against the chandelier-rattling wind.

"It's on the second floor," she said as she led the way up the graceful curved staircase.

Once inside the bedroom, she realized that she was alone. She turned to see James standing just beyond the doorway, staring into the bedroom, his face pale.

"Are you all right?"

He didn't seem to hear her as he stared at the trunk, transfixed.

"Do you need to sit?" Maggie took a step toward him.

"I'm sorry." James shook his head, snapping out of it. "I just remembered something I have to do." Without another word, he turned and bolted down the stairs.

Before she reached the landing, the front door slammed and he was gone.

Maggie stared after him, speechless.

What was that about?

As the storm loomed, Maggie shoved aside her thoughts about James's odd behavior and concentrated on preparing for a possible power outage. She checked flashlight batteries and butane lighters as well as hurricane lamps and antique match holders. In a cupboard near the kitchen sink was a rectangular glass water dispenser that she filled easily using the faucet sprayer. *Very clever, Aunt Evelyn.*

Even as she bustled about, she felt a definite chill in the house. The temperature seemed to have dropped at least ten degrees. In addition to turning up the heat, she layered on her blue fleece pullover and started a fire in the library fireplace.

Satisfied that she'd done all she could, Maggie wrapped herself in an afghan and stretched out on the settee next to the window so she could watch the storm. Once she was settled, Snickers jumped onto her lap and curled up.

As flames licked at the logs and cast dancing shadows on the paneled walls, the wind picked up and whipped leaves past the window. She cuddled her purring cat, who was utterly unperturbed by the raging weather outside.

In the comfort of her warm library, her thoughts drifted back to James. She hoped he'd made it home before the storm hit. He'd rushed from the manor so abruptly, Maggie wondered if he was okay. He'd said he had something to do, but he definitely looked pale. Maybe he was ill. Or maybe there was another reason.

Instead of listing all of the possibilities, she pulled her cell phone from her pocket and dialed his number. She was relieved when he answered.

"Are you all right?"

"I'm sorry for running out like that." His voice was guarded. "I remembered I had to sign for a delivery." He quickly changed the subject to the trunk and gave Maggie a few pointers for its restoration—stripping products, sandpaper grit, finishing options. But it was obvious that his mind was elsewhere.

Not wanting to push, she brought the call to an end as cheerfully as she could. Afterward, she stared into the fire, biting her lip. "Well, that didn't clear things up."

Snickers opened his eyes a bit and nuzzled against Maggie. "Sweet cat," she said as she petted him.

The light drizzle became a deluge, turning the driveway into an aquaduct with water rushing toward the road. She could barely distinguish the yellow fog lights of the cars on Shoreline Drive. When Maggie shifted to get a better view, Snickers jumped from her lap and settled himself by the fire.

Curious to see what the storm was doing to her yard, she went to the back of the house and stood in front of the tall windows in the living room. She couldn't see much besides the lighthouse beam as it slashed through the gray veil of fog. Mesmerized by its rhythm, she watched until a crack of lightning forked across the dark sky and made her jump away from the windows. *Only a squall, indeed!*

While the storm raged, Maggie returned to the comfort of her toasty library and browsed the shelves. She paged through a book about antiques restoration, one on the history of Maine, and a traditional New England cookbook.

As she scanned the shelves, a tome about the Great Depression caught her eye. A colorful bookmark was sticking out of the top. She opened it to find a note in the margin in Aunt Evelyn's handwriting. Text was underlined: *Some men left their families behind and hitchhiked to California in search of work.* Aunt Evelyn had written: *Adam?*

Who was Adam?

Suddenly aware that the sounds of the rain had stopped, Maggie peered outside. Tree limbs were scattered around and the drainpipes gurgled. The sky was pale gray and free of dark clouds.

I guess it was only a squall.

Feeling restless, she went into the office. Most of the crates and boxes she'd seen on her first day in the manor still lined the walls. The room was more for storage than a home office these days, and Maggie couldn't tolerate the clutter.

Before Emily was born, Maggie had managed the office for the dean of the English department at Bennington College. She'd had that department running like a top—handling schedules, keeping a team of absentminded professors on track, and helping students navigate the complicated university system. If she'd been able to whip that place into shape, she had no doubt she could tackle her aunt's mess. It was time to get started.

Maggie sat down behind the flame mahogany pedestal partners desk, the centerpiece of the room, and opened a drawer. Reviewing its contents, she tossed grocery receipts, expired coupons, and old mail. From the next drawer, she threw away ancient bank statements and outdated paperwork.

When she'd had enough, she gravitated to her aunt's journal, a chronicle of the antiques she had found and their histories. Maggie had already discovered that her aunt had invented her own shorthand. For example, if there was a star on the page, that could mean a sheriff, a movie star, or something celestial. It could also mean that Aunt Evelyn was fond of doodling the night sky.

As she leaned back and stretched, her mind went straight to the humpback trunk she was going to restore. She wanted to uncover its history. It struck her how alike she and Aunt Evelyn were in that regard. She smiled, visualizing her diminutive aunt sitting behind this big desk in a chair that surely would have swallowed her small frame.

Maggie wrote a reminder on her notepad: *Move crates.* To amuse herself, she put a star next to it.

With renewed determination, she opened another drawer and pulled out one folder after another. They were all labeled *Miscellaneous.*

Maggie laughed and shook her head. Maybe she was done with organizing for the day.

She thought about going outside to clear the driveway of sticks and check on the Carriage House. Since it was Monday and the shop was closed, June McGillis, the shop's manager, wouldn't be there to assess any damage.

It occurred to Maggie that she should call and check in with June. She picked up the old-fashioned phone in the office and dialed June's cell number.

"I wanted to let you know not to worry about the shop," Maggie said when June answered. "I'm going down to check on it in a bit."

"I'm here already," June said cheerfully. "I should have called to let you know."

"Did you survive the storm all right? No flooding or broken glassware?"

"We're fine. I've got a few buyers coming in today, so I decided to open." She lowered her voice and added, "We've even got some customers."

After checking that June wasn't in the middle of a sale, Maggie continued. "I'm wondering if there's room in the shop storage for these crates that Aunt Evelyn has over here in the home office. Do I need to give you a few days to figure it out?"

"There's room. I'll have to shift some things around, but I've sold quite a bit, so I could use the inventory. We'll need to do some serious buying pretty soon for the holidays. Is that something you want to handle, or would you like me to do it?"

"You know what the customers want, so I bow to your expertise."

"Not a problem. I've got my eye on a few auctions."

"I'd love to join you and learn how the business operates. Will you let me know when you plan to shop?"

"Absolutely. I'll keep you in the loop."

"Wonderful." Maggie tried to sound upbeat, although her heart was breaking for June. She knew it couldn't be easy to manage the shop while dealing with her grief. June and Maggie's Aunt Evelyn had been close friends. Maggie resolved to be more present to fill in for her aunt's absence.

"That's solid walnut," she heard June say to a customer. "Hold on a sec, Maggie."

Snickers leaped onto the desk and batted at the twisty phone cord. The old landline phone was typical of Aunt Evelyn's whimsy. Maggie gently diverted the cat's attention by distracting him with a pen, one of his favorite things to knock to the floor and bat into hidden corners.

When June came back on the line, Maggie asked, "Do you have regular movers, or should I check the directory?"

"You've met Robert Linton, the police officer. For simple jobs like those crates, his son, Bobby, and Bobby's friend Jarrod can move them easily. They're in high school, but they're reliable and not as expensive as the professionals I use for the more fragile items like china and chandeliers."

"If you think they're good, I'll call them."

"They're nice kids. Football players and Eagle Scouts. Evelyn used to let them camp out and do nature walks on the Sedgwick property."

Maggie could hear rustling noises that told her June was flipping through her list of contacts.

"Here it is." June relayed Bobby's cell phone number. Then they made a loose plan to get together to discuss the holiday buying strategy in more detail.

Maggie was grateful that June was staying on at the antiques shop. She didn't know what she would do without her.

After they hung up, Maggie called Bobby Linton, though she wasn't sure she should phone during school hours. Emily's high school had had a "no cell phone" policy, but Maggie knew that some districts now encouraged students to bring their own technology to class and take advantage of it as a learning tool. She was thankful when the call went straight to voice mail; she'd hate to be the person who interrupted chemistry lab.

With that out of the way, Maggie went into the kitchen to heat up some clam chowder to have for lunch with her homemade sourdough bread. While it heated, she returned to the office and tried again to locate notations about the humpback trunk in Aunt Evelyn's journal—if she'd listed it at all. Maggie still hadn't figured out why some things were mentioned and others weren't.

The trunk had been in the manor when Emily was a toddler. So if she could locate an entry from fifteen years ago, all she would have to do was search backward and find a description that mentioned vaudeville stickers. *Easy enough.*

To get her bearings, she opened the journal to the first page. Aunt Evelyn had begun her notes with a list of all of the pieces that were in Sedgwick Manor when she purchased the place. She had it itemized room by room, but there was no mention of what was in the attic. Had she simply not gotten around to it? The attic was a huge space. It wouldn't be unusual for some item to go unnoticed for years.

Maggie had to admit that she found the attic intimidating and creepy. It was only her love of the elegant clothes tucked in the many trunks, wardrobes, and chifforobes that had drawn her there as a child. She didn't recall Aunt Evelyn ever accompanying her there. She wondered if the attic had spooked her aunt too.

Unless it was absolutely necessary, Maggie decided, she wasn't going up there. The sad-eyed mannequins were downright ghoulish. As a child, she'd once dreamed that they came to life at night and roamed the house, looking for her. It took some time to get over that childhood phobia.

With a sharp meow, Snickers alerted Maggie that her clam chowder was ready for him to try. She went back to the kitchen, spooned out a small amount for the cat, then served herself while his portion cooled. When she set it down, Snickers gave it a sniff and then walked away; although, Maggie noticed that he returned to it after she started eating.

"That was very polite of you to wait."

As she was sopping up the last of the chowder with a piece of bread, Bobby called during his lunchtime at school to say that he and Jarrod would come by later that day to move whatever she needed. "The rain's passed, so we'll have no problem using an open truck bed."

They agreed on a time, and she hung up the phone, feeling optimistic. Nice teenagers filled her with good cheer.

· · · · · · · · · · · · · · · · ·

By the time school let out that day, the only remaining signs of the storm were the wet roads and shimmering trees that glistened like diamonds against the mid-afternoon sun.

Bobby and Jarrod were strong kids, and they had no problem loading the humpback trunk from the upstairs bedroom and the crates from the home office. Maggie watched as Bobby drove the truck slowly out onto Shoreline Drive and down to the antiques shop.

In the time it took her to lock the manor and walk over to the shop, they had already put the boxes in storage and the trunk in the workshop. Maggie wrote each of them a check and promised to call again when she needed anything else moved.

After the boys left and the Carriage House was empty of shoppers, June strode to the door and poked her head outside. "No customers." She turned and hustled toward the back of the shop. "Let's have a cup of tea."

Slim, with short, strawberry-blond hair, June was five years older than Maggie. Today she was dressed in casual dark pants with a stylish ruffled French blouse. The cloisonné ballpoint pen on a chain that she wore around her neck—a gift from Evelyn—swung as she walked purposefully into the workshop to make their tea in the kitchenette.

Maggie sat at the Duncan Phyfe table that was part of a dining-room vignette and looked around at the antiques shop. Rather than a hodgepodge of items, June arranged the antiques in settings she called "vignettes" that demonstrated to the buyers how each thing might fit into their homes. The shop was decorated for fall with pumpkins and gourds, colorful leaves and dried corncobs, apples and cranberries. It brought back fond memories of when Maggie and Richard used to take Emily on hayrides.

In minutes, June returned with two mugs of orange pekoe tea. The women relaxed together and chatted amiably about the inventory, their holiday needs, and their daughters. Maggie understood why Evelyn had trusted June so completely. She was practical and professional about the business while being passionate and enthusiastic about the antiques.

When they were done with their tea, Maggie leaned back and stretched. "I want to pull that lining out of the trunk today. I'll sand it first before replacing the fabric. But I'm anxious to see if that old trunk is as solid as I think it is." She told June how it had gotten gashed so many years before. "I'm glad I have the chance to repair it. If I find out its history, I might write it up on a card to keep with it." Maggie didn't intend to leave frustrating mysteries for her heirs to solve.

"You're not getting rid of the stickers, are you?" June asked.

"No way. They're part of its charm."

June, who was trained in furniture repair and restoration, gave her advice on how to remove them temporarily without any damage.

Maggie jotted down the instructions in her notepad. "Did Evelyn ever tell you where she got the trunk? I haven't found any comments about it in her journal so far."

"She never mentioned it to me." June shrugged. "It's been in that bedroom for as long as I can remember."

"Do you think it's authentic?" Maggie reached out to take June's empty mug. "From the vaudeville era?"

"I do."

That cheered Maggie a bit. If it wasn't a reproduction, she felt confident that Aunt Evelyn would have mentioned it in the journal.

Back in the workshop, she washed the mugs in the porcelain farmhouse sink. By the kitchenette was a cozy office area with a rolltop desk, copier, and computer. She sat in the supple leather swivel chair and surveyed the room.

Overall, the space was warm, with antique industrial pendant lights that hung at regular intervals and enhanced the late-day sun streaming through the row of windows. Neatly labeled woodworking and upholstery tools of every description filled the paneled wall above the worktable that now held her vaudeville trunk. Underneath the table were baskets of batting and assorted needles. On either side of the worktable were cherry cabinets with lots of little drawers filled with hardware, fixtures, and decorative bits. Rough-hewn wooden shelves were stocked with cans and bottles of varnishes, oils, polishes, and stains, their labels clearly displayed.

Maggie stood and took a breath, detecting the pleasant aromas of wood shavings, mineral spirits, and furniture polish. As she crossed the room to the worktable, she noticed the broom and dustpan that hung by the door, a reminder to keep the floor as clean as she found it. She imagined June did everything she could not to track sawdust into the shop.

At the worktable, she ran her hand along the scratch on the trunk and thoughts of Emily sprang to mind. Maggie had never been so excited for Thanksgiving. She'd get to see her daughter, and maybe they'd start a new tradition of having holidays at Sedgwick Manor, away from Bennington and the painful memories of the sad times after Richard's death.

The loss had been difficult, but they were getting used to it. Maggie supposed she would also get used to not having her daughter around.

Regular emails and calls after church on Sundays were no substitute for Emily's daily presence in her life. Maggie had no idea how tough the curriculum would be for a first-semester freshman in the nursing program. But Emily was smart and disciplined. She'd do fine.

I'm not sure how I'll handle it though.

Pulling the work stool closer to the table, she perched herself on it and opened the trunk lid. Slowly she eased the lining away from the wood. The material was fragile from age, but if she was careful, she could use it as the perfect pattern for the new lining.

James had told her there were reproductions of these old fabrics. She'd meet with him soon to see the swatches—*if he's actually okay.*

Maggie squinted intently at a rumpled spot in the fabric. The bottom edge of the lining was loose. She worked her fingers inside and tugged lightly. It pulled away, and she began to understand the simple satisfactions of furniture restoration.

"What in the world . . . ?"

A folded piece of paper the color of eggshell had been stuck behind the fabric lining. Maggie pulled it out carefully. It had the velvety feel of aged vellum, and it smelled musty. She unfolded the page and saw that it was a letter. It was dated September 20, 1930. The handwriting was distinctive, bold, and neat. But it was the ink itself that caught her attention.

The letter looked like it had been written in blood.

3

A chill crept up Maggie's spine and the hairs on the back of her neck prickled as she stared at the paper. It was as if someone were speaking to her from the grave.

How long has this paper been hidden in here?

Her thoughts whirled with images of prohibition-era speakeasies and gangsters in felt hats. The letter had been written in 1930, which meant the Great Depression was in full swing. If she remembered correctly, at that time, "talking" motion pictures were new and vaudeville was pretty much dead.

It began, *Dearest.*

A love letter!

Had it been tucked away by a lovesick girl? Or perhaps it spoke of forbidden young love, hidden from prying parental eyes. Smiling, Maggie smoothed the crease and read:

Dearest,

I count the days until my return to your loving arms and to welcome our child into this puzzling world. Being apart these months has been difficult. I had so hoped to build our nest egg, but a musician's pay has been disappointing.

She glanced up at the colorful vaudeville decals on the trunk's exterior. One in particular caught her eye—The Palace Theatre. So, it had belonged to an actual performer, a musician. *What a wonderful piece of history to add to this old gem!* She continued reading:

I do not believe that vaudeville can survive. We are reduced to performing only between reels. The pay barely sustains my needs. This brings me to confess that I have done a terrible thing, my love.

Maggie covered her mouth, intrigued at what might follow. The 1930s were desperate times. Picturing destitute people standing in soup lines and sleeping in doorways, she read the next few lines:

Schuler offered me a substantial amount of money to drive him and his friend. It was not until the next day when I read about it in the newspaper that I learned it had been for a bank robbery.

A bank robbery? The words brought to mind John Dillinger and Baby Face Nelson, machine guns and merciless men. It made her blood run cold.

I had unknowingly become a getaway driver. And now I am a wanted man. I refused the money. Schuler told me not to go to the police, but

Maggie turned the sheet over but saw no more writing. She pulled away the remaining lining as quickly as she could, hoping to find the second page of the letter, but she found nothing.

She shivered and wrapped her arms around herself. How tragic to think that an innocent young man had been duped into becoming a criminal.

Could this writer be one of my ancestors? Did Aunt Evelyn know?

For a fleeting moment, she flashed on James's odd behavior and wondered if he knew anything about it. *But that would be ridiculous. He couldn't possibly be aware of a hidden letter from 1930.* She was sure, however, that he had been looking directly at the trunk before he'd dashed from the house.

Maggie refolded the note and went into the shop to show June.

"I found something interesting in the lining of that vaudeville trunk." She handed over the paper. "Interesting and terrible."

"I'm on to you, Maggie," June said, a twinkle in her eye. "You sound like Evelyn when she got obsessed with a particular piece. She loved to uncover its secrets."

"This one's a doozy." Maggie gestured to the page. "It's about a bank robbery in 1930."

"Fantastic! I have some customers who collect ephemera like that." June's eyes widened as she read. But before she could respond, the chime on the front door rang out and June went to help the couple who had just entered the shop.

Back in the workroom, Maggie inspected the letter. It looked authentic, but she had read about people aging paper in the microwave and then selling the documents as antiques.

I almost hope this is a fake.

She found an acid-free protective sleeve in the rolltop desk and slipped the delicate old paper into the envelope, reasoning that her aunt would have done the same if she'd known about it.

June stepped into the workroom. "They're gone, but I've got a decorator coming by any minute. If you want to authenticate that letter, you might ask James. He could look at it or recommend an expert. He knows everyone in the area who's in the business."

James's strange reaction to the trunk came to mind again, but Maggie dismissed it. If anyone knew how to preserve a piece of ephemera, she knew it would be James.

The front entrance bell rang out and June opened the door between the showroom and the workshop. Maggie caught a glimpse of a woman wearing a black wool skirt, red jacket, and knee-high boots. She had breezed into the shop with an air of confidence that identified her as a regular.

"That's my appointment." June waved a greeting to the woman and then turned back. "You could also ask Ruth if you can't get ahold of James."

Ruth Harper, president of the historical society, was one of Maggie's new friends in Somerset Harbor. At sixty-four, she was extremely knowledgeable about the area and its residents. After a little bit of a rough start, Maggie and Ruth had bonded over their shared interest in history and antiques, and their affection for Maggie's Aunt Evelyn.

After her awkward conversation with James, Maggie decided that Ruth was the better choice to ask about the letter, so she left a brief message on her answering machine before returning to the manor.

Maggie found Snickers on her bed, and she joined him for some quality snuggling time. While she was giving him belly rubs, her eyes settled on the safe where she kept all of the important papers she was now in charge of, mostly documents pertaining to her recent inheritance. She decided that was as good as anywhere else in the house to store the letter.

After placing it in the safe, she straightened the throw she kept over the metal box and then centered the vase she kept on top.

Not in the mood to cook, Maggie went to the kitchen and grabbed a frozen meal of meat loaf, mashed potatoes, and peas from the freezer. She had made it the week before and portioned it out for herself into individual servings. It was hard to cook for one, so she finally decided she would continue to make the same recipes she had used when she had an active, growing daughter to feed. She found that she liked having a stash of ready-made meals. It certainly made her life easier.

As she and Snickers ate, she paged through the newspaper.

A quick look at the weather forecast convinced her that she should plan a trip to Vermont immediately. November in New England had a history of freezing mornings, occasional snow, and winter storms. She needed to retrieve her winter wardrobe soon if she planned to spend more time at Sedgwick Manor.

The idea of a trip to Bennington didn't thrill her as much as she thought it would, but that was probably because she was excited to restore the trunk and figure out who had written the letter that had been hiding inside. Also, she was getting used to life in Somerset Harbor. It was hard to remember how she had filled her days in Bennington without an estate to take care of and an antiques store to enjoy.

After dinner, Maggie settled into her favorite chair in the library to finish reading a mystery novel and sip her peppermint tea. She was engrossed when the phone rang and startled her back into reality.

"Hi, Mom. I have a head cold, and my ears are clogged." Emily didn't sound well at all. "I was driving everyone nuts in class, sniffling and blowing my nose." The phone muffled, and Emily sneezed three times in rapid succession. "My roommate is the messiest person in the whole world, and all her clutter keeps spilling over onto my side. It's disgusting. And her snore is like a lion's roar. I need earplugs—except not right now because—*achoo!*"

"You can always move here. The daily commute wouldn't be bad."

"In the winter? No thanks."

Maggie hadn't really thought that commuting was a good idea. She wanted her daughter to get the full college experience. "I'm going to Bennington in a few days. Do you need anything other than your heavier clothes? You can pick them up at Thanksgiving."

"Thanksgiving?" There was a muffled hacking cough and a long pause.

"Go to the campus clinic. Get something for that cold." Maggie hated the fact that she couldn't be there to take care of her daughter.

"Okay. I have to go. Love you, Mom." In the middle of another cough, the phone went silent.

Maggie felt the motherly urge to jump into her car and roar off to Standish to retrieve her baby girl. But Emily wasn't a child anymore. Stepping aside to let her daughter take care of herself was more difficult than she had imagined.

As she stared at her phone, thinking she should call Emily back and tell her to drink plenty of fluids, it rang, giving Maggie such a start that she nearly dropped it.

It was Ruth calling her back.

"I think James is really the best one to ask about antique documents. He's done a lot of restoration of maps and vintage railroad timetables. He's pretty good at spotting fakes too. He's sort of our jack-of-all-trades."

There's no getting around it. James Bennett is the man for the job.

Maggie's first order of business the next day would be to head to The Busy Bean. James always stopped there after his morning run, so she was fairly certain she would bump into him. She'd bring the letter and get his expert opinion.

In her bedroom, Maggie dug in her aunt's closet for a bag to transport the letter without bending it. She found a slim leather zippered bag that would fit inside her purse. Then she pulled the envelope out of the safe and slid it into the bag.

She hoped that the impromptu meeting with James would dispel any lingering awkwardness between them. It was hard, navigating the choppy waters of making new friends, and it had been a long time since she'd had to.

. . . .

Before breakfast, Maggie shrugged into her windbreaker, said goodbye to Snickers, and braced herself against the cold wind blowing off the water as she walked briskly to The Busy Bean.

The bell above the door jangled as she entered the café, and Daisy looked up from her conversation with a customer seated at the counter. Today she wore her mane of hair in a bun at the nape of her neck, secured with chopsticks.

"Hello, sweet lady," Daisy greeted Maggie in her rich Southern drawl. She was quick to remind anyone who dared tease her about her accent that there was no way the word *harbor* should be pronounced "ha-bah," the way locals said it. She was also insistent that *y'all* was short for "you all," the plural. Apparently no true Southern belle would ever use it as a singular reference.

Daisy's Miss Savannah win had garnered her a full scholarship to college, where she had earned a master's degree in business administration. In addition to owning and running The Busy Bean, she also managed her husband Harry's business, which had grown from one lobster boat to a fleet of three under her guidance.

Although their four children were grown and elsewhere, a family portrait hung in the coffee shop, along with the Miss Savannah sash and crown. Daisy dismissed the display as another lifetime ago. "It's a conversation starter for the tourists," she said, although it didn't seem as if Daisy ever needed any help being sociable.

James was seated at the counter and grinned at Maggie as she entered.

"May I join you?" she asked.

"Certainly. Do you want to sit at 'our' table?"

"We have a table?" Maggie teased, relieved that whatever had happened between them appeared to be over.

"I hope so. I'm getting a plaque engraved." James quirked an eyebrow at her. "I was going to put it on one of the tables by the window. I know how you like to look outside."

"That's true, but doesn't everyone?"

James shrugged. "I think most of us are only vaguely aware of the view."

While he went to get their coffee, Maggie looked around the busy café. He was right. No one seemed at all interested in the view, although she couldn't imagine that happening to her. The shoreline was endlessly fascinating. Even the storms like the one yesterday had beauty.

James brought over two mugs and slid into the seat opposite her.

"Can I get your professional opinion again?" she asked.

"Shoot."

"Was it common for people to use reddish brown ink for correspondence in the first half of the twentieth century? I mean, for personal letters."

James put down his mug. "I suppose bankers, brokers, and accountants used red ink for deficit items. But for correspondence, not really. Is it a dark reddish brown?"

She thought for a second. "Yes."

"It was probably originally black but faded with age. The pigments they used then didn't hold up as well as they do today. Of course, forgeries are common. Do you want me to take a look at it?"

"Sure." She opened her purse, and the coffee turned to acid in her stomach as she peered inside. "It's gone!"

4

Maggie squeezed her eyes shut. She distinctly remembered retrieving the letter from the safe in her bedroom.

The bag. The zippered bag with the letter was still lying on her nightstand.

"I forgot to put it in my purse." She groaned and shook her head. "Sorry about that. If I don't leave myself a note—"

"That's okay," James said. "We can do it another time."

"When I get back." Maggie sipped her coffee.

"You're leaving us?"

"I'm going to Bennington to get my winter wardrobe. I'm sure people are tired of seeing me in the few outfits I brought."

"I'm not."

In response to that comment, Maggie took a long sip of her coffee.

"Bennington's museum has the largest collection of Grandma Moses paintings in the world. I'd like to see it. Would you mind if I tag along?"

Surprised, Maggie hesitated. "It'll be an overnight trip."

"That's okay with me. I could help if you need to carry any heavy boxes or appraise anything."

"I hadn't planned on doing any buying on this trip."

"I meant I could help appraise your belongings. For when you put your house up for sale."

Sell the cottage? Maggie hadn't resigned herself to giving up the home where she and Richard had lived their entire married lives and where they had raised Emily. She pictured the doorjamb between the dining room and the kitchen, where the measurements of their daughter's growth were recorded.

"Selling the cottage hasn't really been in my thoughts. I've been so overwhelmed." She flushed slightly. "But I'd be glad for the company and your help. That's a very generous offer. And everyone should have the opportunity to see the museum. It's small, but lovely."

He leaned back in his chair. "The next few days are pretty clear for me, and what plans I do have can be changed."

"If June will look in on Snickers, I was thinking about going tomorrow. Would you be able to make that happen?"

"I can." James grinned. "That's the beauty of working for yourself. You don't have to clear it with anyone."

"Must be nice. I have to run all of my travel plans by the cat." Maggie rose, reaching for the bill.

James snatched it up before she could look at it. "I believe it's my turn to pay."

"Come to think of it, you're right." Maggie swung her purse over her shoulder. "Maybe you can buy off Daisy with one of those charming smiles of yours."

"I save them for high-ticket items, like hitching rides to Bennington." James flashed her a big smile.

Maggie laughed. "I'll call you after I talk to June."

She waved goodbye to Daisy and braced herself for the wind, wondering if the warm, lazy summers she remembered as a child had really happened, or if they were only a part of her fantasies, like hidden tunnels and secret rooms.

When Maggie got home, she took the letter from the bag and put it back in the safe, still mad at herself for forgetting to bring it to show to James.

She settled into the breakfast nook with an English muffin and checked her calendar against her running list of things to do. She started a new list for Thanksgiving preparations, then checked the newspaper classifieds for any interesting possibilities to increase inventory at the shop. After breakfast, she headed to the home office and made a few phone calls to auction houses to join their mailing lists.

Since she was already in the office, she gave in to the temptation to research the trunk again by diving back into Aunt Evelyn's journal of acquisitions. Within an hour she had located the entry describing the vaudeville-era piece. It was followed by one cryptic sentence:

Some stories are best left untold.

What in the world did that mean? Maggie exhaled slowly. She had hoped that finding what she was looking for would have been more satisfying.

She knew that Aunt Evelyn and Uncle George had honeymooned in New York City, where The Palace Theatre was located. Maybe they had purchased the trunk at an auction house there.

Had Evelyn known the letter was hidden away in the lining?

She put down the journal and decided to go to the workshop and take another look at that trunk.

What story is best left untold?

. . . .

The Carriage House was pleasantly crowded with early-bird Christmas shoppers and people making upgrades to their decor in preparation for holiday guests. Maggie put the trunk out of her mind and pitched in, chatting with customers and offering information where she could.

By noon the shop had emptied, so Maggie and June took a break in a pair of Eastlake armchairs in a sitting-room display, a walnut William and Mary candlestand between them.

"Are you having any luck getting information about that

letter?" June asked. "I've talked to a few collectors who usually go for pieces like that, and some of them are interested in seeing it."

Maggie felt her heart skip a beat. "Maybe it's best not to mention it to anyone else just yet. The subject is pretty sensitive, and it could be awkward if one of the descendants still lives here."

Some stories are best left untold.

"Right, of course." June mimed closing her lips, locking them, and throwing away the key.

"I'm probably being overcautious." Yet her aunt's diary notation made her feel uneasy.

June shifted in her chair, which meant that at any moment, she would probably pop up and start dusting something. Maggie took the opportunity to talk about her plans to return to Vermont for a few things. Before she could even ask, June offered to look in on Snickers.

"Will you have help in Bennington? I'm sure you've got a lot to pack up."

Maggie wondered how much stuff June thought she was bringing to Sedgwick Manor. And then it occurred to her that she should really set herself up for the winter, beyond clothing. It was possible that bad weather would prevent her from traveling to Bennington for weeks on end.

"James is coming along to do some of the heavy lifting. He also wants to see the Grandma Moses collection at the museum."

June smiled. "I'm glad that you two are friends. It's good for him, poor thing."

"'Poor thing'?" Maggie never would have classified James Bennett as a "poor thing." "He's always so cheerful. And everyone in town seems to love him."

"We all tease that he's the nonstick bachelor. A good number of women have tried to catch the golden ring, but their fingers slip right off." She lowered her voice and leaned forward. "This was before I moved to Somerset Harbor, but I heard he was engaged. Something terrible happened, and they say it changed him."

"How long ago?" Maggie couldn't keep the astonishment from her voice.

"At least ten years or so. Maybe longer."

As deeply as Richard's death had affected Maggie, she felt she could now carry the pain without it adversely affecting the rest of her life, and it had been only three years.

"That's the rumor," June said as she stood. She pulled a rag from her back pocket and swiped it over an amber oil lamp.

"Well, anyway," Maggie said, "I'll cancel the weekly house-cleaners, so there won't be any traffic to the manor. It would probably traumatize Snickers to have strangers there while I'm gone, and I don't want to chance him getting outside."

Snickers was still on edge, getting used to such a big space. Maggie had to admit that she was too. *Can animals "catch" anxiety from their humans? But who wouldn't be jumpy with all the creaks and groans?* Logically she knew that those "footsteps" in the attic at night were from the house settling due to the changing temperatures, but she'd gotten into the habit of wedging a chair under her bedroom doorknob when she went to bed. She vowed to curb her imagination in the future, for her own peace of mind as well as her cat's.

Maybe when some of our things are moved to Sedgwick Manor, we'll feel more at home.

· · · · · · · · · · · · · · · · ·

With everything arranged with June, Maggie and James were able to get an early start for Bennington the next day. She was grateful to have company on the trip. She pushed June's comments about a tragic loss in his past from her mind and kept the conversation light, focusing on antiques and Somerset Harbor.

Time passed quickly and soon Maggie's Jetta was stopped in front of the museum in Bennington. James was planning to spend the afternoon there.

"I'll check into the hotel later," he said as he opened the car door to get out.

"It's a block that way." She pointed.

"Grandma Moses, here I come." James wished Maggie luck and stood on the curb until she pulled away. When she glanced in her rearview mirror, she saw him waving to her.

Once she was alone, Maggie felt more apprehensive than excited about facing the task ahead of her. As she pulled into her driveway, she was almost nervous.

She and the cottage had become estranged. The trellis that had held dozens of pink baby roses last summer hung askew. The soft beige exterior looked sickly next to its forest-green shutters.

She hesitated at the front door as if waiting for an invitation to enter. An unpleasant stuffy odor assaulted her nose when she stepped inside. The house was cold and as quiet as a crypt.

But as she passed photos on the wall from Emily's childhood, she was inspired by her daughter. It seemed so natural for teenagers to move on, grow, and learn new skills. Change was inevitable for everyone. There was no time to be maudlin about it. She tied up her hair and got to work.

Maggie started with the hurricane lamp that matched the one in what was to be Emily's room in Sedgwick Manor. She took it apart, wrapped it in paper, and set it in a box. Next, she pulled her framed nautical samplers from the walls and boxed them along with family photos and scrapbooks.

In the bedroom, she went straight for the closet and surveyed her clothes. That little black dress with sequins still had the tags on it. She'd bought it for a faculty Christmas party right before Richard had died. Maggie fingered the material, remembering when the sight of it could bring on a flood of tears. Then she plucked the hanger from the rod and tossed the dress onto the bed. *Who knows what this new chapter of my life will hold?* Maybe she would host grand parties at the manor.

After she bagged up her clothes, she repeated the packing process in Emily's room. She went to the hall closet and filled bags with down coats, wool hats, gloves, and more scarves than any two women should own. She considered getting rid of some things but decided that was a project for when she was snowed in at the manor.

Once she had the bulk of their things ready to load into the car, she wandered through the house and scrutinized her remaining belongings. In the den, she sat down in front of her old desktop computer. She was almost surprised when she pressed the power button and it hummed to life. *Maybe I should pack this thing up and take it home.*

Maggie froze, slack-jawed. Had she just called Somerset Harbor *home*? Had she really crossed that unmarked threshold? Without even realizing she was doing it, she had embraced change.

She sat back and watched the screen brighten. The wallpaper on the computer had been set by Richard. It was a photo of the four of them—Maggie, Richard, Emily and Snickers—on the back porch. Richard had taken it with his phone, his arm stretched out. He'd unsuccessfully taken about ten in a row, so by the time he'd gotten a photo with everyone in the frame, they were crying with laughter.

But that cheerful, loving home was gone. It had been for three years. Maggie didn't want it to turn into a grumpy widow's cottage where their happy memories got lost to time.

That settles it.

She would contact a realtor friend before leaving and put the cottage on the market. Perhaps someone on the college faculty would want it, or maybe a graduate student. She'd suggest that the realtor contact the college first and see if they were looking for any new property. She liked the idea of guest lecturers staying there.

Realizing that darkness had fallen, Maggie called James's cell phone.

"My cupboards are bare. How do you feel about dinner?" she asked.

"I could eat," James answered. "Care to join me at the hotel restaurant? Their menu looks good."

"I'd rather take you to The Four Chimneys Inn. They have a great lobster ravioli." She stopped short. "What am I thinking, telling a Maine native about lobster in landlocked Vermont? They have rack of lamb with lemon mint glaze that's amazing. And there's a very good braised vegetable plate too."

"Stop. You're making me even hungrier. Let's go soon."

"Give me half an hour." Maggie thought a quick shower was in order after having spent the day kicking up dust.

"Perfect. I'll watch for you from the lobby so you don't have to park."

On the way to James's hotel, Maggie realized that she knew very little about him. Shouldn't she know simple things, such as if he ate meat? She knew he liked apple pie and had a tragic past. *Well, that's unsubstantiated.*

She brushed the rumor aside. Maggie wanted to get to know James without any preconceived notions. She thought all new friendships deserved as much if they were to have a chance.

At the restaurant, Maggie enjoyed listening to James's reactions to the Grandma Moses collection and the remarkable items such a small museum had amassed. "Come spring, I'll return the favor by taking you to the museum in Rockland," he said. "It has work by all three of the Wyeths—Andrew, N.C., and Jamie."

As they waited for her fillet and his rack of lamb, Maggie learned that James enjoyed old Hitchcock movies. By dessert she'd discovered that they shared a love of key lime pie. Although these revelations weren't earth-shattering, she felt as if she knew him a little better.

When they parted for the night, James promised to help her load the car and pack anything else she missed the next day.

Back at the cottage, Maggie rolled herself into the double wedding ring quilt that her grandmother had made for her birth. "Hello, old friend. It hasn't been the same without you."

She lay still, listening intently for any familiar sounds, but she heard nothing. In the deafening silence, her thoughts refused to shut down. She drifted to Somerset Harbor and the humpback trunk.

Why did Aunt Evelyn, usually so eager to share the histories of her antiques, keep the story of the trunk to herself? Was it too awful to repeat?

5

The next morning, Maggie had breakfast in the hotel restaurant with James before he went to the cottage with her to help her pack.

"I'm expecting a call from my realtor." Maggie gestured to the landline phone. "If it rings, would you mind answering it? Give me a yell. I'll be in the attic."

She left James packing her china and went to see what she needed from storage. Maggie felt her heart flutter when she spotted the decorated shoe box atop a container of summer clothes.

She sat on the attic floor and opened it. Inside were the love poems Richard had sent her all throughout college. Rarely did they rhyme without strain, but they spoke of his feelings for her, and she cherished them.

She closed the box, clutching it to her, recalling the secret letter tucked in her safe. *Did that young man write other letters to his sweetheart?*

The shrill ring of the phone downstairs brought her back to the present. She grabbed the clothes and the box and hurried down the steps.

"Was that the realtor?" she asked.

"I don't know. They hung up when I answered." James picked up a stack of boxes and walked them out to the car.

Looking at the call history, she saw Emily's number. She phoned back immediately, but it went to voice mail. Maggie left a message that she was clearing the cottage of personal belongings and would call her when she got back to Sedgwick Manor. "Take care of yourself. You're precious to me."

After they packed the Jetta, Maggie set off for Maine. Along the way, she pointed out landmarks and covered bridges to James, aware that she was moving away from the familiar and toward her new home.

"I'm anxious to finish the vaudeville trunk before the holidays are upon us. Did Aunt Evelyn ever mention it to you?" she asked.

"Not that I recall." James opened a map. "Do we go through St. Johnsbury? I read about a dog chapel there that sounds interesting."

She shook her head, too distracted to ask what a dog chapel was. She had a lot of thoughts competing for her attention. In one corner was the trunk she was puzzling over, and in the other was the cottage she was leaving behind. Now she thought that she probably should have told Emily before putting the house on the market.

Realistically, though, her daughter would never again live with her full time. When Emily finished her studies, she would go where her career opportunities took her. She was full of big plans for her life. Her options were many, what with all the specialties available in nursing. Her daughter was so sure of her own bright future that it was heartening.

At some point, that young letter writer in 1930 also must have thought the world was his oyster. But events like the Depression, coupled with his own naivety, had changed his life forever.

"You seem a million miles away." James's voice cut through her thoughts. "Would you like me to drive for a while?"

"No, I'm fine." Maggie sighed. "I was wondering how Emily will take the news that I put the only home she's ever known up for sale."

"If you're uncomfortable with the idea, you might think about leasing it on a yearly basis until you and Emily are ready to let go of the place," he suggested. "That way you don't have to make the decision right now, but the house doesn't have to sit empty, and you can make some money from it."

Maggie hadn't realized that she was smiling until James asked her why.

"Not once since I've known you—or any of my new friends in Somerset Harbor—have you told me what I need to do," she replied. "After Richard died, people in Bennington started telling me how to live my life—move to a condo, get my master's and teach, go work at the college. Worst of all, they kept trying to get me into something they called 'the dating pool.' Well-intentioned, I'm sure, but ill-advised. I suspect I might have drowned."

From the corner of her eye, she saw James nod. He no doubt had gone through—*and may still be going through*—the same thing.

"At any rate," she continued, "I appreciate your suggestion, because it made me realize that I made the right choice. It's time to move on from the cottage. It looks like Somerset Harbor is my home now."

"Now you have to register to vote there."

Maggie burst out laughing. "Of course. You're not going to let me forget that, are you? Election's coming up in the spring, isn't it, Alderman Bennett?"

"Actually, I'm not up for reelection until next term. But I think of it more as a responsibility to my town than some coveted honor to campaign for. If the people don't think I'm doing a good job, I'm happy to step aside."

"You'll have to tell me who's who in this election. I've seen some political ads around town recently."

"There's an ordinance against plastering those things on town-owned light poles and parking meters." James sounded irritated.

Maggie shot him a quick look, surprised by his tone.

"They detract from the beauty of our little village." His voice definitely had an edge to it. "I want the residents to be proud to live in Somerset Harbor, and I want tourists to remember it as a beautiful place to visit."

"There's your campaign speech."

James smiled and relaxed into his seat. "Our town was free of billboards long before Lady Bird Johnson suggested it."

"Someone doesn't care about that ordinance." Maggie tried to recall the name on the posters she'd seen. "A candidate for district attorney, I think."

James made a sound of disgust. "Yes, that would be Jeff Davidson. His election isn't for months, but he's already pouring money into his campaign, which doesn't make a difference to me since I'm voting for Sam Skyler. Still, you'd think someone who wants to be the DA would know better than to break the law. I rip his signs down whenever I see them, but they spring right back up like mushrooms after a rain."

"Speaking of signs, how about a lunch break? I see there's a coffee shop at the next exit."

He agreed, and Maggie drove them to a small, cheery place off the highway in New Hampshire, a pretty good find for a roadside stop.

The conversation remained fluid and fun as they had coffee, sandwiches, and pie. In fact, Maggie enjoyed every minute. It was easy to see why everyone in town loved James.

When the bill came, he grabbed it. "I've got this."

Naturally, they argued over it.

Maggie pointed out that James had come along to help her, and she wanted to thank him.

James said he'd hitched a ride to see a museum, and he wanted to thank *her*.

In the end, James won by waving the bill in his hand. "Possession is nine-tenths of the law." He leaned forward and whispered conspiratorially, "Their pies don't compare to Daisy's, do they?"

"Not even close."

Back in the car, Maggie steered the conversation away from politics. "I thought some of the shops in town would close in the colder weather, but I've been surprised to see that tourists keep coming. The Carriage House actually operates in the black every month. I suspect some of that success is from your recommendations."

"That's all June," he said. "She and Evelyn were a great team. June cultivates a loyal following of professional designers and decorators. It's really sharp the way she keeps her regular customers informed the moment she gets something she thinks they might like."

"Good to know." Privately, though, Maggie wished that June hadn't been so eager to share the news about the letter. "I want to learn the business, but I also want to leave the everyday stuff to June."

"Almost all the shops in town are one-person operations," James told her. "Fran Vosburg manages to teach and have quilting bees while keeping a steady inventory on hand at The Quilt Cupboard."

"I absolutely fell in love with one of her quilts. It's got a peony on it. Its petals form the whole quilt. Very unique. I hope it's still there when I go back. It's incredible."

"Thanks. I'll tell my mother you said so. If it's gone, I'm pretty sure she'd make another for you."

"Your mother?"

"Another talented Somerset Harbor native," James said, "like her son."

Maggie laughed. "I've never heard anyone mention her before. She's the one who creates those fantastic hand-stitched quilts that Fran sells?"

"Just the nicest ones." He puffed out his chest comically.

"I would love to meet her."

"She's not very social," James said quickly. "She doesn't go out."

Maggie had read of people who feared leaving their homes. It was such a stark contrast to James, who was on friendly terms with most of the town. *What interesting extremes his family has.* She was about to press him for more details, but something stopped her.

. . . .

It was after sunset when she pulled in front of his apartment. "Thanks for your help and your company."

"You're welcome. Thanks for letting me join you. I'll talk to you soon." Before he closed the car door, he added, "We'll get that fabric you need."

As she pulled away, she was acutely aware that she'd only learned a bit more about James than she knew before. She liked him though. He actually listened, which was a rare trait. She didn't want to mess up that friendship by getting too nosy.

Maggie felt her pulse quicken as Sedgwick Manor came into her view. The word *home* ran across her thoughts again.

A bit stiff from the long drive, she decided to unload the car to get the kinks out. She didn't like sitting for so long. She popped the trunk, grabbed a bag of clothes, and headed for the front door.

Inside, she flipped the switch, and the crystal chandelier flooded the foyer and hall with light.

Snickers's mew sounded like a combination of "I'm glad you're home" and "What took you so long?"

She squatted, dumped the bag on the floor, and opened her arms. The cat made a flying leap for her shoulder, nearly knocking her over. Maggie embraced the vibrating ball of fur. "Did you miss me?"

After she properly apologized for leaving him all alone, she made a quick call to June to thank her for taking care of Snickers.

"I got him some treats. I left them in the cupboard by his food."

"That was so nice of you." Maggie noticed that her cat looked like he had put on a little weight recently. "You didn't have to do that."

"Well, I think Snickers would disagree with you. He insisted I give them to him when I arrived and when I left."

Maggie chuckled. "He's going to wish I never returned."

After hanging up with Snickers's new best friend, she emptied her car. Maggie stashed Emily's clothes and belongings in the upstairs bedroom facing the ocean. She was sure her daughter would enjoy the view when she came for Thanksgiving, and having her things here would help her feel at home.

Then Maggie stored her dishes in the china hutch. With their rope edges and tiny flowers, they weren't quite as grand as the Baroque-era bone china that had belonged to Aunt Evelyn, but she loved the pattern. They would do nicely for less-formal occasions.

She carried her table linens, including the set of holiday bread covers she had cross-stitched, to the butler's pantry, and she stored the bed linens in a closet upstairs. Then Maggie put her cross-stitch and Swedish huck pattern books in the library.

At last, she grabbed her quilt from the backseat of the car and carried it to her room. She spread it across the bed, and Snickers leaped up, purring and rubbing his whiskers across it. He rolled over and flattened himself against the blanket, writhing contentedly.

"I missed it too."

Officially exhausted, she dressed for bed and slid under the covers with Snickers settling close to her. The weight of the quilt was like a hug from her mother and grandmother. In the dark, she pictured the familiar designs of the fabrics. It was comforting to know that Grandmother McCrary had skipped off to school in the red gingham that made up part of the quilt and that pieces of her mother's wedding dress were stitched into the entwined rings.

After she married Richard, she had continued the tradition, contributing material from her own wedding dress. Alas, the true quilting skill in her family had ended with her mother's death ten years ago.

Her last thought before she fell asleep wasn't of her own family though. It was of James's reclusive mother. *Curious.*

· · · · · · · · · · · · · · · · ·

Maggie awoke early, refreshed but worried about Emily. She wished she could go to St. Joseph's and bundle her up, feed her chicken noodle soup, and make her some tea. She longed for Thanksgiving to come sooner. A simple meal would be nice for their first holiday together at Sedgwick Manor. But she didn't want it to be too simple. Some of their favorites would have to make it on the menu.

Instead of having breakfast at home, she dressed and headed to The Busy Bean. If anything important had happened while she was out of town, she'd get the scoop there.

As she neared the coffee shop, Maggie was startled out of her thoughts by a stocky man with a staccato accent that sounded more Brooklyn than New England. He wore an expensive-looking suit and loafers, and he reeked of fancy cologne and new money.

"Are you old enough to vote, young lady?" He flashed a disingenuous grin. "If so, I'm your man." He shoved a postcard emblazoned with his photo into her hand. *Make Davidson your next DA.*

She instinctively drew back, feeling as if she were a fly about to be pulled into a spiderweb. *Who does he think he is, trying to flatter me with that corny line?*

He winked. "As a newcomer, you could do worse than to have the DA as a friend."

Her eyes widened in surprise. She wondered how he could

possibly know that she was new to town. She was about to ask when she realized that his focus had already shifted elsewhere. Now he directed his phony smile beyond her shoulder, where a couple of attractive young women were walking toward them.

Pushing past her, he extended his hand. "Young ladies, you couldn't possibly be old enough to vote, but tell your mommy to vote for Davidson."

Maggie crumpled the card as she slipped through the door of The Busy Bean, but not before she noticed a new sign on it: *This is a politics-free establishment.*

Inside, Daisy wagged fingers adorned with emerald-green nails at her. "You met him, huh? He's slicker than calf slobber."

Maggie laughed. "I missed you."

"How was Bennington?" Daisy drawled as she filled a mug and slid it over.

Maggie raised a questioning eyebrow. Was her trip the latest subject of town gossip? *Of course it was.*

"I officially put my cottage on the market. Other than that, it was *uneventful.*" She placed slight emphasis on the final word, knowing what Daisy was really curious about.

"Aw, honey, that's too bad." Daisy turned her lip into a pout.

Shaking her head, Maggie changed the subject. "Is the library within walking distance from here?"

"It's up this side street a couple of blocks. Run out of mystery novels?"

"Not really." The moist heat rising off the coffee felt good. "I'm hoping to solve a real mystery today."

The case of the unsuspecting getaway driver.

Maggie chuckled at her first glimpse of the town library—a white two-story building that resembled the hull of a dry-docked boat with porthole-style windows in double rows. Inside, navy blue carpet not only muted any sounds but also continued the nautical theme. Recessed lighting kept it bright and cheery.

The children's section, with miniature chairs and tables, was in the front. One wall featured a bulletin board decorated with crayon drawings of stick figures in yellow slickers, rain boots, and red umbrellas. Maggie smiled wistfully, remembering when her refrigerator had proudly displayed Emily's drawings of starry nights and sunny days edged with smiley-face stickers.

But it was a different kind of sticker she wanted to look for today. The vaudeville decals on the trunk had intrigued her, and she was on the hunt for information about them or a vaudeville musician from Somerset Harbor.

At the front desk, Maggie filled out her request for a library card and then headed to the nonfiction section. She bypassed the history books and went straight to the newspapers to look for articles about a local musician from that era.

The librarian had told her that the newspaper files were incomplete, but what they had would be on microfiche in the cabinets that lined the rear wall. As she approached, a shelf of Somerset Harbor High yearbooks caught her eye.

It struck Maggie that she and James probably graduated from high school in the same year, and she slid the yearbook off the shelf to see what her friend looked like when he was a teenager.

She was hoping to find something to tease him about—a bad haircut or an unusual hobby. But what she found was an earnest, all-American boy.

James had been a member of the Honor Society, the first-string quarterback, and an Eagle Scout. His senior class had voted him the most popular boy in his year. *No surprise there.* His air of confidence had apparently set in early, or maybe he aggressively overcompensated for his nearly invisible mother by making himself especially visible.

Maggie paged through the yearbook and found a photo of James with his arm around a girl; both were in formal clothes and wearing crowns. He and Natalie Boarder were listed as the most popular couple as well as prom king and queen. She was as beautiful as he was handsome.

Could Natalie have been his fiancée?

Curiosity got the better of her. She put the yearbook back on the shelf and selected a few microfiche boxes of *The Somerset Harbor Herald* that were likely to mention his engagement. Sure enough, in an edition from the year after their high school graduation, Maggie found a glamorous photo in the society pages that announced Natalie's engagement to James. They must have been barely nineteen and in their freshman year at college. She wondered how the Boarder and Bennett families had felt about that.

Without giving too much thought to her motivation, Maggie continued to scan the newspapers. She paused on a few stories about locals she knew and the Boarder family. They seemed to have been Somerset Harbor royalty, given all the feature articles about their charities and the many photos of them on the deck of their yacht and Natalie with her catamaran, *The Golden Girl*.

She noticed that James had disappeared from the news after his graduation.

Maggie couldn't help but compare the Boarders' wealthy, glamorous lifestyle with what she imagined it was like to grow up with a mother who either couldn't or wouldn't socialize.

The next mention of Natalie made Maggie gasp. Aware that several people nearby had glanced curiously at her, she faked a cough and continued reading. It wasn't the social pages that had caught her attention, but a headline on the front page above the fold: *Socialite Natalie Boarder Lost at Sea.*

Maggie was enveloped in an icy chill. Suddenly she felt embarrassed as she realized she was acting like a busybody. Conscience told her to shut off the machine, yet she felt that she had to know more. *What a horrible tragedy.* To lose a loved one was always terrible, but young love made it all the more heartbreaking.

The article mentioned that the couple had been seen arguing on the dock before they went out in the catamaran. Although a storm had been predicted for later that day, the warning flags weren't flying when they left. But the storm hit sooner than expected, and the couple failed to return.

The Boarders called the Coast Guard to search, and they eventually towed *The Golden Girl* to shore. Natalie was missing, and James was incoherent when questioned by the police.

The stricken fiancé said that Miss Boarder was not deterred by the weather warnings and insisted on going out. When Bennett failed to persuade her to remain onshore, he went with her.

The grieving parents had demanded that James be charged with negligent homicide, but the investigation was "inconclusive." Natalie's body was never recovered.

Maggie's heart ached for what her friend and the Boarders must have gone through. But had Natalie's parents really thought that James was to blame? Or had they simply needed to lash out at someone?

She searched through the archives for follow-up stories. It had been big news in this little coastal town for several months following. The paper carried copies of the police reports and texts of press conferences.

Natalie hadn't been wearing a life vest when she was knocked overboard by the boom. James dove into the water again and again, searching for her, and very nearly drowning himself while the catamaran traveled some distance in the choppy waters.

The memorial service was months later, after the Boarders finally accepted the drowning as official. James wasn't listed among the mourners. She imagined that he had been unwelcome. It would have been horrible to not only lose your loved one but also to receive so much animosity from her family.

June was right. Something terrible did happen.

Maggie turned off the reader and replaced the fiche in its jacket. How doubly tragic that James had been taken to the police station for questioning by his friend Robert Linton, who had gone to the police academy and joined the force right out of high school. James had gone from being half of the "golden couple" to being accused of homicide by his sweetheart's parents—all in an afternoon.

Bleary-eyed and disquieted, she decided to save her vaudeville research for another day. On her way out, she stopped by the front desk to collect her new library card along with a voter registration form to fill out and turn in at the courthouse. Maggie tucked them into her handbag and pulled out her list.

While she was out, she thought she might as well pick up a few items at the little grocery store in town. She needed a bag of kibble for Snickers, and she was in the mood for a turkey sandwich with cranberry sauce for lunch. Thanksgiving couldn't come soon enough. And she thought beef stew sounded good for dinner, if that wasn't too disloyal to a coastal town noted for its seafood.

She loved being able to run all of her errands on foot—coffee, library, grocery store—although she thought she might eventually have to get herself a little shopping cart.

As she was waiting for her sandwich at the deli counter, she felt a hand on her arm. It was Ina Linton, Robert's aunt and a true authority on everything in Somerset Harbor. A tiny but hardy woman, her face was pink beneath her thinning cotton-white hair. Weather permitting, Ina walked everywhere—"unless it's raining bobcats and dingoes"—which probably explained the excellent health of this seventy-five-year-old woman.

She wore an outfit similar to that of a Venetian gondolier—a red-and-white striped shirt and black pants under her bright red fall jacket. Maggie half expected her to break into an aria at any moment.

Ina smiled up at her. "I heard that you've made it official and put your Vermont home up for sale."

Small towns certainly had speedy grapevines. Maggie made a mental note to call Emily as soon as possible. She didn't want the news to reach her somehow before they had a chance to talk.

As the older woman was ordering a lobster roll, it occurred to Maggie that Ina might know something about the vaudeville trunk.

"Would you like to come to the manor and eat lunch together?"

"Absolutely," Ina said without hesitation. "I'll meet you at the front of the store. I've got a few more things to buy."

Shameless, Maggie scolded herself as they left the grocery store together a few minutes later. Of course she enjoyed Ina's company, but her ulterior motive was to see what she could learn from her.

"Bobby told me you've cleared the office of crates," Ina said. "I bet it looks the way it used to now."

Amused that such trivia had not escaped Ina, Maggie nodded. "And I brought some of my personal items from Vermont to add to the mix." She figured that would be a good bit of news Ina could contribute to the town conversation. "I have some cross-stitched nautical samplers I want to put in one of the upstairs bedrooms. They're perfect for a seaside setting."

"Get rid of some of those outlandish botanical prints Evelyn favored." Ina didn't break her brisk stride as she spoke.

Maggie tried to keep up, wondering if Ina had ever mentioned that opinion to Aunt Evelyn. They'd been good friends, so she could only imagine the lively discussions between those two.

Back home, Maggie filled a kettle with water to heat for tea while Ina settled in at the kitchen nook and fussed over Snickers. "Evelyn and I always sat here together. She was a stubborn old bird," Ina said good-naturedly.

"She used to tell me, 'If you're not a little stubborn, people won't know what you stand for.'"

"But not too stubborn. Evelyn didn't get herself stuck in ruts." Ina unwrapped her sandwich and laid it on the deli paper, refusing the plate Maggie offered. "Once she tried to get fancy and serve us high tea in the library. I said, 'Who do you think I am? The queen of the harbor?' She started calling me 'Queenie' after that."

Maggie laughed. "I like the library, but I don't usually eat in there. I'm afraid I might spill something and the captain will disapprove." She knew that the portrait was part of Sedgwick Manor's history, but she wished it was someplace else—like the courthouse. She grinned, imagining its effect on anyone at trial.

As the women ate their sandwiches, they talked about Evelyn, the historical society, and the erratic coastal weather until Maggie felt comfortable mentioning what was really on her mind.

"I found a humpback trunk with vaudeville stickers on it in one of the spare bedrooms upstairs, and I was wondering about its history. Do you remember stories about vaudeville performers from here? Wasn't there a local musician or two who played The Palace in New York City?"

Ina took a big bite of her sandwich and didn't reply.

Maggie pressed on. "Schuler? What was the other one's name?"

The second hand of the kitchen clock made a steady ticking. Finally, Ina spoke. "You've heard the old saying about sleeping dogs? This is one of those situations where it's best not to poke at them."

"So you do know something."

Ina gazed out the window as she nodded. "Evelyn told me about that trunk when she started looking into it. Then nothing. So I asked how it was going." The older woman's face darkened. "I remember her expression when she told me she'd stopped looking. I think she discovered something . . . dangerous." Ina picked up her teacup in both hands but didn't drink from it. "If Evelyn Bradbury wouldn't touch it, my advice is to leave it alone."

Maggie's lips tightened. "I appreciate you telling me this. But if you remember anything else—"

The older woman patted Maggie's hand, then stood. "This has been nice, but I've got things to do before the storm hits. It's stalled in Canada for now, but it'll get here eventually." Ina wrapped herself in her jacket. "Oh, before I forget, Evelyn has boxes of decorations and ornaments for Thanksgiving in the attic. She went all out in the fall, with pumpkins outside and even a Thanksgiving tree. I don't know anyone else who ever decorated a tree for Thanksgiving." She chuckled. "She saw life differently than most of us."

Maggie stood at the door, watching Ina as she walked briskly to Shoreline Drive. Had Aunt Evelyn found the letter, investigated it, and then replaced it in the trunk? It seemed unlikely that her keen-eyed aunt had missed it, and Ina's story supported this theory.

What's going on with this thing?

Back in the kitchen, as she got her stew started in the slow cooker, she called Emily.

Her daughter answered on the first ring.

"How's your cold? You sound better."

"I am. The campus clinic gave me antibiotics, and the fever was gone pretty quickly. I'm down to a rattle when I cough, which I can handle. I don't think I could have made it without my quilt."

After the usual catching up, Maggie steeled herself to deliver the news. "I've really been enjoying living at Sedgwick Manor, and I've decided to stay. It was a hard decision to make, but it seems silly to hang on to the cottage in Bennington. So I'm putting it up for sale."

Maggie heard Emily catch her breath, but she said nothing. "Sweetheart?"

"But that's our home!"

"I would have told you sooner, but it all happened pretty quickly."

"Where were you when I called the house?" Emily's tone suddenly sounded frosty. "Who was that man who answered your phone?"

"That was James Bennett. He's a friend from Somerset Harbor. He offered to appraise some items and help me move boxes." Maggie felt her cheeks flush and changed the subject. "I didn't have room for your bicycle. It's time we got you a better one anyway, if you want to ride."

There was more silence on the other end of the line.

"You've got a beautiful room at the manor with a view of the ocean." Maggie tried to soothe her daughter. "You'll see how nice it is when you come for Thanksgiving."

There was a long pause before Emily answered. "About Thanksgiving . . . I need to stay on campus. Finals start right after the holiday. I've got papers due and tests right up until they let us out for Christmas."

"Oh, you poor girl." Maggie tried to hide her disappointment. "I'm sorry you have so much to do in such a short time." It hadn't occurred to Maggie that her daughter wouldn't be able to get away for the holiday. But she remembered vaguely how stressful finals were, mostly from when she worked at Bennington and the harried students would shuffle by her office wearing pajama pants, eyes barely open.

"And getting sick set me back." Emily sniffled.

"Tackle it bit by bit. And remember to take breaks and sleep enough." That was the advice her father had given her when she called home overwhelmed. It must have worked because she'd made it through college and had a history degree to show for it.

"I've gotta go. I'm meeting my study group at the library." Emily hung up before Maggie could respond.

She stared at the silent phone.

She's not coming for Thanksgiving?

7

Maggie stood in the middle of the kitchen feeling at loose ends.

It'll be our first holiday apart.

By rote, she finished her stew for the slow cooker, her daughter's pain and the cancellation of their holiday together weighing heavily on her heart.

Snickers rubbed against her legs, but even her sweet cat couldn't make her feel better. She hated to think about Emily upset and alone at school.

Without anything else to do in the kitchen, Maggie went to the library, plopped down, and picked up the paperback mystery she had started recently. The portrait of the captain glared down at her.

"I agree." Maggie glowered back at him.

She attempted to lose herself in the story but put the book down after the damsel tumbled from her horse right into the arms of the obvious villain.

"Why am I reading this ridiculous mystery when I have a real one to solve?"

Snickers, who was curled up on the back of the settee, didn't have an opinion. He stretched and joined her as she went to her sitting room, where she'd left her laptop.

She wanted to find out more about the vaudeville decals from the trunk. Even if Aunt Evelyn's warning was true that the story was best left untold, it couldn't hurt to do a little historical research.

After countless searches and clicks, Maggie was grateful for the distraction when James called.

"If you're not busy, I thought we could meet for coffee and then walk to my place to choose a fabric for the lining of that trunk you're refurbishing."

"That would be great." Maggie had already closed her laptop and gotten to her feet. "I can leave in a few minutes."

"No rush. I need to make my afternoon rounds at The Bean."

Before she left, Maggie opened her bedroom window and sprinkled dried kernels of corn and peanuts onto the sill outside. "There, Snickers. You can watch the birds while I'm out." The blue jays and crows had quickly learned that the cat behind the glass was no threat to them. In fact, they seemed to enjoy having an audience.

In the full-length mirror, Maggie checked to see if she was put together enough to go out in public. She found that she felt more ragged than she looked. After a little primping, she noticed that Snickers was also grooming himself. "Always look your best, right?" The tabby gave his paw another lick and stretched lazily.

Even after brushing her hair and pinching her cheeks, Maggie thought she looked a little drab, so she looped a colorful fringed scarf around her neck. *Not bad.*

. . . .

James was already at the café when she arrived. Ever the attentive alderman, he was talking cheerfully to another patron.

Daisy looked up from behind the counter. "Hi there, pretty lady. The usual?"

Maggie felt comforted, realizing that her friend knew her so well already, but maybe it was time to take a page out of Aunt Evelyn's book and add a little mystery to her image.

"I think I'll try your Jamaican blend today, no cream. To go."

Daisy gave an approving look but didn't offer a comment.

With her cup in hand, Maggie and James left The Busy Bean

together, something she was sure Daisy would mention to her at some point.

"Nice scarf," James said as they strolled down Shoreline Drive.

"Thanks." She touched the fabric at her neck, suddenly self-conscious. "Richard got it for me when we were on a dig in Peru. We watched the artisan finish it and take it off the loom."

"You went on digs?"

"A few."

"That must have been amazing."

"It was." Maggie took a sip of her coffee. "That was before Emily. After she was born, Richard switched to urban archaeology so he could be local. There's still a lot left to uncover from the Revolution and before."

James nodded and then pointed to the sky, which had turned a light purple. "Looks like that storm's rolling in."

"Finally." Darker clouds were creeping over the horizon, in no particular hurry as far as Maggie could tell.

"There's still plenty of time to choose a swatch and get back home," James said with authority.

"You coastal people really know your weather." Maggie was already paying more attention to it, seeing that it was the local pastime.

James's apartment was above his office and had a spectacular view of the ocean. It was decorated in midcentury modern furniture, something Maggie didn't expect.

She was able to identify the Knoll tulip chairs around the pedestal dining table. In the living area, he had a white leather Barcelona chair and a black Herman Miller sofa, probably both replicas. Aunt Sharon—Evelyn's polar opposite—had similar tastes, so Maggie had a passing familiarity with the designs.

"Considering your preservation work, I would never have figured you for modern."

"The apartment came with most of this furniture already here. My landlord called it 'old junk.' Can you imagine?"

Maggie considered the possibility that all of the furniture was authentic.

"He told me I could get rid of it or keep it. So I cleaned it up, repaired a few pieces, and went with it." James shrugged. "I like it well enough, but if I'm ever run out of town again, it'll be easy to leave behind."

Run out of town again? Maggie furrowed her brow at him.

James finally gave a little laugh. "I'm kidding." He waved it off and then gestured to the boxy leather sofa. "Have a seat. I'll get the sample books."

As he disappeared down the hall, Maggie's cell phone rang. She looked at the caller ID and saw it was Emily. "I have to take this," she shouted out to him.

She didn't want to add insult to injury by having Emily overhear James in the background. She suspected her daughter wasn't upset only about the sale of her childhood home, but also because her mother had a male friend.

"Mom, I'm sorry." Emily hiccupped the way she did after a cry.

"I'm sorry too." Maggie paced James's living room.

"Of course you should sell the cottage if you're staying in Somerset Harbor. It makes sense."

Maggie exhaled a sigh of relief. "It'll be sad to say goodbye to our home though."

"But we can bear it." Emily was repeating what her mother had often said at the peak of their grief over Richard's death. "I know Dad's in our hearts, not in the cottage." Emily's voice caught for a second, but she recovered. "And I'm sure it must be hard for you to live there by yourself."

Maggie felt herself choking up at her daughter's empathy.

"I love you, Mom. But I really do have to go."

"I love you too."

With that, Emily was gone.

As Maggie blinked back her tears, she noticed she was holding a framed photograph that she'd absent-mindedly plucked from the side table by the sofa. She focused her eyes on the sepia print.

A little boy, about three years old, dressed in a cowboy costume, sat straddling a humpback trunk, probably pretending it was his horse. With the same smile and eyes, it had to be James. His chubby little leg was nearly covering something.

If she hadn't been so familiar with it, she might not have recognized what it was. She couldn't believe her eyes. There was no mistaking it, though.

Right there, by the boy's leg, was the edge of a vaudeville sticker . . . *her* vaudeville sticker on *her* trunk. This was the very same humpback trunk that had languished in Sedgwick Manor for years and was now in the workroom of the Carriage House Antiques shop.

Maggie hastily replaced the photograph when she heard footsteps coming down the hall. She stepped away from the side table and tried to look casual.

James appeared with two sample books in his arms. He gave no indication that he thought it was odd to see his friend standing stock-still in the middle of his living room. He plopped the samples on the coffee table, sat, and flipped open the top book.

Maggie perched on the other side of the sofa, her mind churning. *I have to ask him about it. Don't I?*

"**A**re you okay?" James stopped paging through the sample book and cocked his head toward Maggie.

What? How does he know I found out about the trunk?

"Was that Emily?" he prompted.

Of course he's not talking about the trunk.

Maggie had been so concerned about getting caught with his photograph in her hands that she had forgotten that her eyes were probably glassy from the tears she'd refused to cry.

"I told her about selling the cottage."

He nodded sympathetically. "Change is hard."

"She took it well, eventually. She's a good kid."

After James got Maggie some water and she told him more about her conversation with Emily, they settled in with the samples.

"I thought this one with the fleur-de-lis might work." It had a golden background with a warm brown design, almost identical to the lining she had removed.

Maggie agreed that it was a good choice, and James showed her a few of the fabrics he'd rejected. Trying to look natural, she leaned back and casually plucked the photo off the side table.

"Is this you?" she asked, pretending that it was the first time she'd ever seen it.

"Yes." James kept his eyes trained on the swatches. "Adorable, wasn't I?"

"Oh, wow!" She was aware of how forced her voice sounded. "It's my vaudeville trunk." She angled the frame in his direction. "The very same one."

Taking the photo from her, James studied it.

"See that small bit of decal behind your leg?" Maggie pointed. "I'd know it anywhere."

He shook his head, looking incredulous.

"You don't remember that trunk?"

"No." James handed the frame back. "Actually, I've always disliked that picture. I keep it because my mother gave it to me, but it gives me the creeps for some reason."

She studied the photo for a moment before replacing it. "You look like you were really enjoying yourself."

"I never gave it much thought." He closed the sample book he was looking at and centered it on top of the other. "When I look at it, I get the feeling that something awful is about to happen."

"Maybe you got stuck inside. That would be scary for a little kid."

"I don't know." His usual charm was gone, and he didn't meet Maggie's eye. "Do you want me to order the first one I showed you?"

"Yes, please. Maybe I'll type up a little history about vaudeville at The Palace Theatre to keep with the trunk for my grandkids' grandkids. If I can find a playbill, I'll include that too."

James nodded, but he was clearly distracted. "You should probably get going. You don't want to be caught in the storm. Would you like me to give you a ride home?"

"No thanks. I'm a fast walker." Maggie tried to force a pleasant farewell smile, but she was taken aback by the turn of events.

Outside, the cold air stung like a slap to her face. She didn't need a psych degree to assume that James had experienced some type of childhood trauma that he preferred to forget.

But what could it possibly be?

She hated to imagine, so she attempted to push her thoughts away. She had no business opening old wounds. Yet the questions lingered.

With a glance to the darkening sky and roiling clouds, she turned toward the library. She wanted a book or two on vaudeville to keep her company during the storm.

Maggie rushed into the already-empty building and selected the most promising books. She sat at one of the tables and hurriedly flipped through the illustrations.

A quick browse of the text confirmed what the letter had said. Talking pictures had sounded the death knell for vaudeville. Musicians and performers were suddenly anachronisms in their own time, although some—like W.C. Fields and Will Rogers—were able to salvage their careers by getting work in the movies.

Did the letter writer slip away to Hollywood? Or did he go to the police, as the letter suggested he would, and wind up in jail for his honesty? The answers had to be somewhere. If not in Somerset Harbor, then perhaps they were recorded on a police blotter tucked away in the basement of an old building or buried in a newspaper archive.

Clearly, James wouldn't be any help in her quest. He couldn't even explain his reaction to the trunk—or he wouldn't. But he had seemed to genuinely not remember.

It was possible that his family only had the piece for a short time before they sold it to Aunt Evelyn, unaware that a stranger's letter was tucked inside the lining. Whatever the case, that letter was part of the trunk's story. Whether it was a triumph or a tragedy remained to be seen.

Maggie jumped at the hand on her shoulder.

"Ms. Watson, right? Storm's coming." The librarian, Maura O'Brien, glanced up at the dark purple sky through the porthole windows. "We're closing early. Looks like there might be some flash flooding."

Maggie checked out, and Maura slipped the book inside a plastic bag for her.

As she hurried through town, her thoughts raced from the hidden letter to the storm to Emily to Bennington. The wind picked up, and Maggie clutched the library bag to her chest. Mist rolled in off the ocean, and a line of indigo clouds churned on the horizon, playing leapfrog. A lone seabird raced for shelter. *I'm right behind you.*

Maggie's bootheels clicked against the sidewalk, which was already dotted with the first large drops of rain. The lighthouse beam sliced through the gray. Fishermen at the wharf were shouting over the wind, hurrying to moor their boats and secure whatever could be tied down. A man in a dark slicker and rubber boots tromped past her as the rain picked up. "Batten down the hatches, ma'am."

The image of Snickers home alone, wind howling and rain pelting, quickened her pace. By the time she turned up the sloping drive, her hair was plastered to her cheek and her pants were heavy with rainwater.

She looked up toward Sedgwick Manor and stopped dead in her tracks.

Is someone in the attic?

In the flicker of light, Maggie was sure she saw the silhouette of a person in the upstairs window. Reacting on instinct, she raced to the manor and unlocked the front door. She considered grabbing an umbrella to wield at the intruder, but she reached for her cell phone instead. "I'm calling the police!" she shouted.

Before she sent the call, a loud bang at the end of the hall made Maggie jump and drop her phone. It went skittering across the floor, and she wished she had that umbrella or something even heavier.

As her eyes adjusted to the dark, she saw that the rear door was open and the wind was battering it against the wall. Maggie ran to it, slammed the door closed, and then leaned against it to catch her breath.

A low, morose caterwauling made her stand straight up.
Snickers!

The sound came from her room. She found him under the bed, tail puffed up and ears plastered against his head. He rushed out and leaped into her arms but then squirmed away when her wet coat met his fur.

"Sorry, Snickers. I guess I didn't lock that door." She forced herself to contradict her gut. "The wind must have blown it open."

Light from passing cars or the lighthouse beam hitting a mirror at precisely the right angle—either one could have produced the mirage of someone in the attic. Add her active imagination to the mix, and she'd panicked.

Rain slammed into the back windows, and a branch of the maple tree made eerie screeching sounds as it rubbed against the glass. Lightning cut a jagged line that stretched from the dark sky to the ground near the stream that ran between the manor and the Carriage House, lighting up the wooden footbridge that spanned it.

Maggie hurried away from the window, Snickers at her heels.

"You're a lucky cat, you know? Think of all the wild animals out there. Where do they go to stay safe?"

A little voice in her head wondered where *she* could go to stay safe.

Maggie slipped out of her boots and shed her wet jacket. She had barely finished changing into comfy pants and her fuzziest sweater when the door knocker clattered. Shoving wet hair from her face, she rushed to answer. Blue and red lights penetrated the gauzy curtains, and she opened the door to see Officer Linton.

"We're checking on a 911 call from here." The policeman stepped inside at Maggie's invitation. "Did you make that call, Ms. Watson?"

"It must have gone through when I dropped the phone. I thought someone was in the house." She felt her cheeks flush. "I dialed but didn't hit Send." She was going to get a reputation for crying wolf if she wasn't careful, and things hadn't turned out so well for that boy in Aesop's story. "I'm so sorry."

"That's all right, ma'am. We'd rather respond to a false alarm than not be here when you need us. Do you want me to check things out?"

"No, that's not necessary. I hate that I got you out in such terrible weather. Would you like some hot cocoa?"

"I need to check the shops along the drive, but thanks." Officer Linton gave a quick nod. "We could lose electricity any time now, so be prepared."

After the officer left, Maggie went to the kitchen and ladled out some beef stew for dinner. When she was finished, she decided hot chocolate with a good dose of mini marshmallows sounded like a good idea.

She felt much better once she was seated in her favorite cozy chair in the library, ready to ride out the storm with her cocoa, library book, flashlight, and cell phone next to her on the side table. Snickers had also calmed down and curled himself atop the fuzzy slippers on her feet. Careful not to disturb him, she pulled a crocheted afghan off the back of the chair and draped it over her shoulders.

Maggie inspected her cell phone. Fortunately, it hadn't broken when she dropped it, so she called June to make sure her friend had made it home from the antiques shop safely.

When she hung up, she became aware of how fierce the storm was getting. Wind whipped the manor, rain hammered the windows, and lightning cast strange shadows on the walls.

Was that what I'd seen in the attic? A trick of the light?

Maggie took a deep breath. "Sorry, Snickers." She wiggled

her toes, and he jumped up. "It's no use. We've got to do it." She wouldn't be able to sleep until she checked the attic.

Armed with her phone and flashlight in case the power went out, she headed up the stairs to the second floor. Snickers joined her, lively at first. But after hearing a high-pitched screech from the wind whipping the house, he stalked along next to her, staying low to the ground.

"It's only the storm," Maggie told her cat in a cajoling tone, but she was acutely aware that she was also trying to convince herself.

At the bottom of the attic steps, she noticed that Snickers had scampered away and was standing a few feet down the hall, looking ready to bolt. "Does that make you a bigger chicken, or smarter than I am?"

His eyes were like twin moons and he didn't budge. He simply mewed sharply.

"Scaredy-cat," she muttered as she mounted the steps.

She ascended quietly, taking one silent step after another, cringing when she hit a creaky stair. If someone was up there, she didn't want to alert him. She'd surprise him and club him with her flashlight.

Maggie turned the knob and cracked the door to the attic, opening it slowly. Inch by inch, she snaked her hand in and felt along the wall. Her fingers found the toggle switch.

She inhaled quietly and held her breath.

In one fell swoop she flipped on the light and kicked open the door, her heavy flashlight raised and ready.

She found herself face-to-face with a man in a dark overcoat, his eyes hidden beneath the brim of a black fedora.

Maggie screamed.

She scuttled back in a panic. Her heart pounded in her chest as she moved quickly to slam the door shut—anything to delay him for a moment.

But he made no move toward her. He made no move at all, in fact.

Her fear-blurred vision cleared, and she let her breath out in relief.

It was only a mannequin, one of many scattered among the steamer trunks, Pullman suitcases, and vanity cases.

Thanks for scaring me half to death, Aunt Evelyn.

She giggled weakly with relief. It must have been the mannequin's silhouette she'd seen. And, as she guessed, the flash of light was likely from the headlights of a passing car reflected by the big mirror propped against the back wall.

If I'm going to sleep tonight, that's my story and I'm sticking to it.

The storm was loud, and it was cold in the attic. A tree branch had shattered one of the windowpanes, and rain was dampening the top of an old cabinet. She wedged a piece of cardboard into the open window and then found a rag and wiped the cabinet. She tried to move it away from the window, but it was too heavy.

She opened the top drawer and saw several boxes marked *Thanksgiving*. Wrapped in tissue were delicate hand-blown glass pumpkins, corncobs, pinecones, cornucopias, and Pilgrim figurines, along with squirrels, bears, and turkeys. A note in her aunt's handwriting said they were for the mantel. A second box had garlands of autumn leaves with pumpkins and gourds.

Maggie smiled. She had been feeling down about Thanksgiving since Emily told her she would be staying at school. It looked like her aunt had given her the solution: make the best of the situation. She decided she would dress the manor to the nines and host a party. It would be a holiday to remember.

Thanks, Aunt Evelyn.

As she descended the stairs, she felt brave and filled with purpose. She had made a lot of big decisions in the past few days, and following Aunt Evelyn's lead on how to celebrate Thanksgiving made her feel particularly bold and independent.

When she reached the landing, Snickers peered up at her with a worried look.

"It's all clear. We're safe."

No sooner had she spoken the words than her eye caught something on the step. She felt as if she had a rock suddenly caught in her throat, choking her.

It was a perfect muddy footprint.

And it wasn't hers.

9

Someone *had* been in her house. What had he been looking for? Sure, there were nice antiques, but there was hardly a black market for nice antiques.

After Maggie collected herself, she came up with a game plan. First, she checked the locks on every window and door while she pointed the beam of her flashlight into all of the dark corners of every room. Then she took a photo of the footprint and put a box over it in case Snickers decided to roam in the night and muss it beyond recognition.

She would call Officer Linton in the morning. If there were any prints outside, they would be long gone from the rain.

For the first time since Emily was a little girl, Maggie checked under the bed before she crawled into it and turned off the light. She pulled the beloved quilt up to her chin as if it could shield her from harm. Snickers pressed his warm, furry body against her neck, comforting her.

They both jumped when the wind shifted and tree branches scraped the window like fingernails across a chalkboard. Endless sheets of lightning illuminated the photo of Emily and Richard on the bedside table while Maggie searched her memory for any possible reason for a man's muddy footprint to be in her house. She could only find one explanation.

Someone's invaded my home!

After she called Officer Linton tomorrow, she would call the locksmith. With that decision in place, she closed her eyes again and tried to sleep. But another scrape from a tree branch against the window jangled her nerves.

And I'm calling the landscaper to get that tree pruned!
Armed with this plan, she eventually fell into a restless sleep.

· · · · · · · · · · · · · · · · ·

When Maggie woke the next morning, the storm was over, leaving standing puddles and the steady gurgling of gutters and drainpipes. She toasted and ate the last of her sourdough bread while she looked out at the glistening pine trees and red maples.

After breakfast, she put together the ingredients for lobster bisque to simmer in her slow cooker. When she was a busy mom, she'd gotten used to doing a lot of slow-cooker cooking. Now that she had more time on her hands, she supposed she could expand her culinary horizons. *Later.* With a Thanksgiving party in the offing, this was not the moment to become Julia Child.

She slipped on a forest-green mohair sweater and jeans, and then called Officer Linton about the shoeprint on her stairs.

She needed to distract herself while she waited for him to arrive. She sat in the office and made a list for her Thanksgiving party plans. She'd decided on an open house, and she would ask everyone in town to come. She went to the drawer where she'd seen boxes of note cards and found a charming handmade set in bold fall colors. Maggie wrote out invitations, feeling exhilarated and nervous. She'd never thrown a party by herself, and she was just starting to wonder if she could pull it off when she saw a police car pull into the driveway.

As she escorted Officer Linton inside, he scolded her for not letting him search the house the night before. "You should have called back."

"This wasn't going anywhere." She lifted the box to reveal the muddy footprint. "It definitely wasn't here before. I would have noticed this."

"Forensics should be able to identify the size and type

of shoe from the tread." Officer Linton snapped photos, took measurements, and made notes. "But until we have a suspect we can compare footwear to, that's about all we can do for now."

After Officer Linton completed his investigation and left, Maggie searched online for a locksmith. She smiled. *What do you know?* There was her landscaper Nate Gregory's name.

He was indeed a man of many talents. She knew from an earlier conversation that during the winter, when lawns were dormant, he pursued his master's degree in horticulture and worked as a handyman. Additionally, he had a Christmas tree farm and pumpkin patch that he ran with his wife, Opal, who owned a cleaning service.

It was still early, but she dialed his number and left a message telling him what she needed.

After she refreshed the food and water for Snickers, she pulled on her puffy winter coat and favorite knit cap, a gift from Aunt Evelyn. She gave Snickers one last scratch under the chin, stepped into the chill, and locked the side door. She shook the knob hard to reassure herself that it was indeed locked and then trotted to the Carriage House to check in with June and get a little work done on the trunk.

The chime sounded as she entered the antiques shop. June looked up from her paperwork with a slight scowl on her otherwise-attractive face.

"You're here early," Maggie said. "Did that storm cause any damage?"

"No. But I saw some fresh marks near the lock on the door this morning. I think someone tried to break in last night."

"They didn't get in?" Officer Linton had mentioned that he was going to be checking all the shops. Maybe the sight of a patrol car had scared away the intruder.

"No. The lock is stubborn even on good days, and wet

weather makes it worse." June held up her hands in surrender. "What do burglars think they can get from here? A Sheraton dressing table?"

"I called the police to the manor last night. They showed up with lights flashing. Maybe they scared off whoever it was."

Eyes wide, June gestured to a matching set of French Restoration mahogany armchairs, and they sat so Maggie could tell her the full story.

"Someone actually broke in? While you were home?"

"Whoever it was must have run out the back when I went in the front, although I can't imagine who it was or why."

"Did you get a look at him?"

"No, but he left a muddy print on the stairs."

"Do you think it was vandals? Or someone taking advantage of the foul weather, hoping to find something valuable to sell?"

Maggie shrugged as she dug her ringing phone out of her pocket. It was Nate.

"I need a new lock for the Carriage House too," Maggie told him after she explained what had happened at the manor. "I'm here now. When do you think you'll be able to come?"

"I'll have to special-order the door locks if you want to keep them authentic looking. They should get here in a couple days."

Maggie couldn't complain. She definitely wanted to maintain the historical integrity of Sedgwick Manor, even if her fear was telling her to get high-tech, fingerprint-coded locks and window bars.

"I'm replacing some damaged storefront windows on Shoreline Drive right now," Nate continued. "I'll come by afterward and take a look at what you have to be sure I get an exact match."

"That reminds me, I have a windowpane in the attic that needs replacing. I put cardboard there, which I'm sure is a soggy mess by now."

Maggie arranged to meet Nate at the manor, and then she went back into the workshop. It was time to get serious about restoring the finish on the trunk. The fabric for the lining would arrive in a few days. As she examined the gash again, she noted that it wasn't as deep as she'd first imagined. She eased the piece onto its back, checking it for any weaknesses that she should repair.

A card was taped to the bottom with a notation in Aunt Evelyn's handwriting. Maggie could have kicked herself for not fully inspecting every inch of the trunk to begin with. She loosened the tape and tilted the card toward the light. It had some of her aunt's inscrutable symbols, but the words were perfectly understandable: *Purchased from Deborah Bennett, 1975. Previous owner Sally Keene.*

Bennett? Could that be James's mother?

If so, then it was proof that it had been his family's trunk after all. Wouldn't he be intrigued to know that his childhood horse had been hiding someone's secret?

Maybe that someone was Sally Keene.

Thrilled to have a name, Maggie intended to find out who she was. Immediately.

She hurried out front and checked in the town directory that June kept behind the counter. There were no Keenes living in Somerset Harbor.

Of course not. That would be too easy.

Disappointed, Maggie returned to the workshop and began sanding, her mind drifting to possible explanations as to how a vaudevillian's trunk could have found its way to Sally Keene, Deborah Bennett, and finally Aunt Evelyn. Had James's mother bought it at a tag sale? Buyers didn't ordinarily keep the names of sellers like that unless they were neighbors or friends—or perhaps kin.

Could it be that Sally was James's grandmother? Her pulse quickened. *How exciting!* She couldn't wait to tell him that the trunk might have belonged to his grandmother. If the trunk had been in his family at least three generations, was it possible that the letter writer was his ancestor?

James had never mentioned his mother's first name, but that would be easy enough to find out. Considering that she sold her quilts through The Quilt Cupboard, Fran would know her.

A sudden thought made Maggie rein in her enthusiasm. Perhaps James and his family did know the secret hidden in the trunk but didn't want anyone else to know.

Some stories are best left untold.

She sighed. Her arms were tired from sanding, though she had switched hands frequently. She dusted herself off and went into the showroom to ask June what she knew about James's mother.

"He's mentioned her in passing, but I don't really know anything about her."

Because she's a recluse.

Back at the manor, Maggie removed her coat and knit cap and hung them on the peg next to the kitchen door. She sniffed the aroma of lobster bisque with satisfaction. It should be perfect by suppertime. For lunch she would have leftover beef stew.

As it heated, she looked for Snickers. He was perched on the back of the settee in the library, staring out the window. He gave her a noncommittal glance before resuming his surveillance of Shoreline Drive traffic.

"Good to see you too," she said.

As Maggie returned to the kitchen, she heard a loud meow behind her. She looked down to see her cat trotting along, looking affronted that she hadn't petted him yet.

"*Now* you're interested. I should get a nice friendly dog that always greets me at the door with a wagging tail."

Snickers butted his head into Maggie's leg when she stopped at the stove to stir her stew.

"Okay, I won't get a dog."

Before she had a chance to put her lunch into a bowl, the phone rang. She turned off the burner and answered, stirring as she spoke.

"Your fabric arrived," James said. "Should I bring it to you this afternoon?"

"That was quick." Maggie was pleased.

"I decided to overnight it."

"Great. Thank you. And I have something to show you." She was thinking he'd be interested in seeing the purchase card. "I'm home the rest of the afternoon. Nate's coming to replace a windowpane in the attic and order new replica door locks."

"Is there something wrong with the originals?"

"I've had a break-in. I wasn't home when it happened, but there's a big muddy footprint to prove it." She tried to sound nonchalant.

"Maybe you should do more than fix the locks. What if you'd walked in on him?"

"I did, sort of," she confessed. "He ran out the back door."

James was silent for a moment. "Did you get a look at him? Anything that might help to identify this person?"

"Unfortunately, no. Although I'm fairly sure it was a man's footprint."

"You need to start carrying pepper spray."

"I thought next time I'd do it the old-fashioned way and douse him with black pepper. Even if he runs away, the police will know him. He'll be sneezing for hours."

"They'll catch him red-nosed."

Maggie laughed, mostly because it was easier to make jokes than to admit how shaken she was.

"It's really bold for someone to roam around a big house like that," James said.

"What makes you think he roamed around?"

"You said there was a footprint, so I'm guessing he didn't stand in the foyer and wait for an invitation."

"Maybe the cat invited him in," she joked.

"You're going to have to train him to be an attack cat," James said.

That made Maggie smile. "Why don't you come by with the fabric around dinnertime, say, about six? I've got lobster bisque and salad. And I'll make fresh sourdough bread."

"It's a deal, if you'll let me take you to church on Sunday."

"I'd like that."

"We could go to lunch after."

Maggie was touched. Her new friends in Somerset Harbor were shaping up to be some of the nicest people she'd ever known. To keep pace, after she ate her lunch, she went to The Busy Bean and got two slices of apple pie for dessert. She'd noticed it was James's favorite.

When she got back to the manor, she wrote out more Thanksgiving invitations until Nate arrived and got to work on the broken window.

While he replaced the pane, she sat atop the steamer trunk and looked around the overstuffed room. The attic didn't look spooky at all in the daylight. She felt silly for having been so scared the night before. Perhaps it was the mannequins scattered among the suitcases and shelves of bric-a-brac. They'd seemed threatening with the lightning casting dramatic moving shadows.

There must be treasures tucked away up here—lots of them. What was the intruder searching for?

She jumped when Nate said, "Good as new. That should

keep out the rain and cold. I'll take some photos of the locks and be on my way."

When Nate was finished, she watched as he pulled his truck onto Shoreline Drive. Before she went back inside, James arrived in his classic black Mercedes. *Perfect timing.*

Maggie had fully intended to show him the purchase note, proof that the trunk once belonged to his family. But as he walked toward the house, a bright smile on his face, she thought of his previous reactions to the humpback trunk.

Suddenly, she wasn't so sure her news would be welcome.

10

The oven buzzer sounded as Maggie let James in.

"That's my bread." She hurried toward the kitchen and pointed to the hall tree. "Hang your jacket and join me."

By the time she set the loaf on the rack to cool, James was standing in the entrance to the kitchen with Snickers sniffing at his shoes. He bent to pet the cat, and Snickers did some prancing for their guest.

"Would you mind eating in here?" Maggie gestured to the kitchen nook. "I feel like I should be serving a five-course meal in the dining room."

"I usually eat in front of the nightly news, so the kitchen is like fine dining to me." James inhaled deeply. "The bisque smells almost as good as the bread."

She smiled. It was nice to have someone to appreciate her cooking.

He set the package on the table. "Do you want to see the fabric now or after supper?"

"We have to wait for the bread to cool a bit." Maggie was excited to see the material.

James opened the box. The beautiful cloth had a pattern that was nearly identical to what she had pulled out of the trunk.

She fingered the loose edge. It was sturdy but pliable. "It should be easy to work with, but if I have any problems . . ."

"What are friends for?"

She forced a smile. *What are friends for indeed?* She had news about a trunk belonging to his family, and yet she was hesitant to share. Some friend she was.

James offered to help put dinner on the table, and she set him to work.

He sliced the bread, and Maggie put the arugula, tomato, and blue cheese salad on the table along with butter and silverware. She gave James a napkin-lined basket, which he filled with sourdough as she ladled the bisque into bowls.

As they ate, Maggie shared her plans for a Thanksgiving open house. James heartily agreed it was a good idea, but he declined her invitation.

"I'm sorry I'll miss it. My mother and I spend the holiday together as a tradition."

Maggie felt a pang of disappointment, but he quickly cheered her up with stories about growing up in Somerset Harbor—baseball games in the summer until it was too dark to see, camping in the woods beyond town with his scouting troop, fishing off the jetty. "I always secretly hoped I wouldn't catch anything."

"You don't like fish?" Maggie asked, her last spoonful of lobster bisque frozen in the air.

"I love it, and I like shellfish even more." He dropped his spoon into the empty soup bowl in front of him. "But I hated taking the fish off the hook."

Maggie laughed as she got up to put the dishes in the sink. When she returned with the apple pie, she took a breath and concentrated on sounding casual. "By the way, when I turned the trunk on its back, I found this."

She pushed the card to his side of the table, and James read it.

"The name Bennett struck me. Is she related to you?"

Staring at it, he cleared his throat. "That's my mother."

"Do you know who Sally Keene is?"

"That was my grandmother. She's deceased."

"Then the trunk was in your family for at least a few

generations." Maggie's pulse quickened. "Evelyn bought it when you were only a few years old, so I could see how you might not remember it."

He said nothing.

"That letter I mentioned the other day—I found it hidden in the lining."

"Really?" James's eyes widened. "I'd like to see it."

"Just one sec." Maggie got up from the table. "I have it in my safe."

When she got back, James was standing in the hallway with his coat on.

"I'm sorry to run out like this, but I had no idea how late it was. I'll barely make my appointment." He glanced at the envelope in Maggie's hand. "I'd love to see that another time. I have a small collection of love letters dating back generations. It could be a nice addition, if you're willing to part with it."

Dismayed, Maggie nodded. He didn't have a clue about the letter. "I'll walk you out."

"Thanks for the delicious meal."

Maggie thanked James for delivering the fabric and then stood in the doorway of the manor, watching him drive away. She closed the door and turned to see Snickers staring at her with his bright, quizzical eyes.

"Well, that didn't go as I'd expected."

. . . .

On Sunday, James picked up Maggie for church. Old Faith Chapel was a small building near the town square. Built in 1731 and one of the oldest churches in the area, it still had the original rough-hewn pulpit.

Little had changed according to the welcome pamphlet. Box pews were divided by two aisles, which was common in New

England meetinghouses. The white clapboard exterior was plain and the bell tower simple, which gave it a peaceful ambiance. The church had originally served the fishing communities that sprang up along the coast. Standing strong against the harsh Maine weather, its modest and sturdy construction perfectly reflected its parishioners.

In the vestibule, clapboard walls held photos of early ships and boats, Blessing of the Fleet ceremonies, and summer regattas. One entire wall was dedicated to those lost at sea. Maggie drifted along, reading the typed explanations with the pictures. She felt her body stiffen when her eyes settled on a photo she recognized from the newspaper. It was Natalie Boarder with her catamaran, *The Golden Girl*.

She froze, not sure what to do.

Standing by her side, James coughed into the crook of his elbow. "Excuse me. I need some air."

Before she could turn around, he was out the door. Maggie wasn't sure if she should follow him or not.

Liz Young, Pastor David's wife, saved her from making that decision. "Maggie, it's so good to see you." She was dressed in a charcoal-gray suit that made her silver-blond hair even brighter than usual. "I hope you're considering joining one of our service groups now that you're settled. I think you might enjoy helping out with our annual tag sale. Your Aunt Evelyn certainly did."

"Definitely." Maggie immediately started thinking of all the things that were packed away in her attic.

"We also take food to shut-ins and run errands for them. That reminds me—David and I serve Thanksgiving dinner every year at the VFW hall. If you're interested, we could always use volunteers."

Maggie told Liz that she would be getting an invitation in the mail shortly for Sedgwick Manor's first Thanksgiving open house.

"How thoughtful of you to invite us," Liz said. "I'm sorry we won't be able to make it."

"You'll have to stop by another time." Maggie was getting used to hiding her disappointment. "And I'd be happy to jump in whenever you need another set of hands to help out with anything."

"That's very generous of you. You're a lot like your aunt."

Maggie took that as high praise.

"I'll give you a call soon." Liz's eyes flashed to her watch, and she excused herself to go to the choir room.

As she stood at the entrance to the sanctuary and scanned the pews, Maggie noticed that James hadn't returned. She went inside and saw Officer Linton motioning for her to sit with him and his family. He quickly introduced her to his wife, Nora. Maggie smiled at their teenage son, Bobby, whom she already knew, as the choir filed into the loft, singing as they took their places.

She recognized some of the faces up there—Ina, Ruth, and Fran. Daisy was front and center, her voice ringing out clear and strong.

Pastor David had no sooner begun the service than a man on the aisle went into a coughing fit and fled the sanctuary. This gave Maggie an opportunity to glance around for James, but she didn't see him.

"The rain fell and the floods came," Pastor David read, "and the winds blew and beat on that house, but it did not fall, because it had been founded on the rock."

Maggie felt blessed to have a home that had stood strong against the storm with no more damage than the loss of a single windowpane. As Pastor David continued, she thought of people who weren't so lucky—the young couple from the letter, struggling during the Depression. She couldn't imagine the hardship and heartbreak they endured.

At the end of the service, on her way out of the sanctuary, Maggie saw James standing near the door.

"Sorry," he said. "I didn't want to cause a ruckus slipping in late. I saw that you were with the Lintons, so I just took the nearest empty seat."

Maggie decided not to mention that she hadn't seen him in the church at all.

Liz had joined her husband at the exit, and the two of them were shaking hands with their congregants.

Pastor David clapped James on the shoulder. "Thank you for getting that pothole out front fixed."

"I'll see you at the next historical society meeting, I hope," Liz said to Maggie.

She agreed, and they moved along with the flow of people into the parking lot.

"There's a great place in town with a nice Sunday brunch menu." James opened the car door for Maggie. "Are you still up for it?"

"If you are, that sounds nice."

The Lobster Quadrille restaurant was in town, but James took them on a detour. "If you go there straight from church, it's packed." So they drove along the coast toward the neighboring town of Seacliff, then doubled back to catch the stunning view from the other direction.

As James pulled into the parking lot, Maggie studied the rustic seaside appeal of The Lobster Quadrille with its weathered cedar shakes, antique sailboat on the front lawn, and hand-hewn sign that bore the restaurant's name. Every time Maggie saw the place, she was reminded of her childhood, lost in the pages of *Alice's Adventures in Wonderland*, where rabbits served tea and lobsters danced.

Inside, the staff wore sailor suits. Charming nautical bulkhead lights with brass rain caps and long bulbs inside wire cages lined the walls. The ceiling had heavy-duty cast-brass navigation lights. A sea chantey played quietly over the sound system as Maggie and James followed the hostess to a table with a view of the ocean.

"I took a quick walk outside of church," James volunteered when they were seated. "That always gets rid of a coughing fit."

Based on his reaction to the photo of Natalie, Maggie highly doubted she was going to hear the story about his fiancée from his lips. She couldn't blame him. She didn't want to rehash the worst events of her life over a friendly lunch on a beautiful Sunday. *Why should he?*

Still, she felt uncomfortable having personal information about James without his knowledge. But he probably knew things about her that she wasn't willing to talk about. That was the way of small towns. Everyone knew everything, but they had the grace not to remind one another.

"Those brass navigation lights are marvelous." Maggie gestured to them. "If they're not originals, they're very good reproductions."

"I was a consultant when they renovated. I located those lights, and they are authentic. I doubt anyone could duplicate the original dings and dents in the brass. It took a lot of sea voyages to give them that used look."

Impressed, she asked him a bit about antique hunting. He recommended a few books for her to read, which led to talk of novels and then upcoming town events.

James sympathized with Maggie when she talked about Emily staying at school for Thanksgiving, and he seemed truly sincere. He didn't minimize her pain or try to explain Emily's point of view, which made Maggie do it herself. "If it'll help her reach her goals, I'm glad to sacrifice a holiday together." In the end, she felt better.

At the manor, James followed Maggie up the steps. She thanked him for the ride and lunch. "I'll probably see you at The Busy Bean tomorrow."

She inserted the key into the front door but found no resistance when she turned it.

A chill slithered up her arms.

"The door's unlocked." Her voice was barely audible.

"Let me go in first," James said. "You dial 911."

Frantic, Maggie burst into the front hall. "Snickers! Here, kitty, kitty!" *What if he slipped out?* He'd already gotten out once and had been terrified after nearly falling into the brook. "Snickers!"

A mournful wail came from her room, and Maggie raced down the hall. "Snickers?"

The lump under the quilt on her bed moved gradually toward the upper edge. First a nose and whiskers, then eyes as wide as saucers appeared.

Maggie scooped him up and cuddled him. "You poor kitty." She smoothed his fur back, and he pushed his head between her arm and body. "It's okay now."

James stood in the doorway with an exasperated scowl on his face. "Someone could have still been here." He put his cell phone into his pocket.

She looked up at him, apologetic. "Sorry."

"I didn't find anyone, and the police are on their way. Until they do a search, we need to stay put."

She noticed for the first time that the woven throw she'd used to disguise the free-standing safe was askew, as if someone had hastily tossed it back on. The vase that had been sitting on it now stood on the floor, and she was certain that the safe had been moved forward.

She wanted to believe that no one had been in her bedroom, but she couldn't explain how the vase would be standing upright if Snickers had been to blame.

It was clear that her intruder had hastily tried to cover his tracks.

Maggie pulled off the throw and saw a dark smudge on the fabric. She looked down at her palm, which was also now dirty. *Where did that come from?*

Upon further examination of the safe, she noticed that there was more grime on the back, and scratches on the metal that hadn't been there before.

"If this thief had gotten my safe open, he would have been disappointed to find a pile of boring paperwork."

And the secret letter.

It might be of interest to a collector, but she doubted it was worth much money. *Would anyone risk prison to steal it?*

Maggie shook it off. A safe usually meant money or valuables. That was all he was after. Someone found out an heiress moved into Sedgwick Manor and figured he'd see what she inherited.

As she scanned the room, however, she noticed that nothing else had been disturbed. Directly in view was an open jewelry box of Aunt Evelyn's, a small treasure chest of valuables, and it appeared untouched.

James answered the door and returned with Officer Linton, whose shift had begun shortly after church.

"Do I get a trophy for most calls in a month?" Maggie joked.

Officer Linton was already assessing the scene. "Have you touched anything?"

"I moved the throw and pulled Snickers out from under the quilt on my bed."

"What's that?" The officer pointed at the cat's paw. "Is it . . . a thread?"

Sure enough, Snickers had a thin shred of material dangling from his paw. "It must have snagged on his claw and gotten stuck when he retracted it."

Maggie held her cat's paw while Officer Linton used tweezers from his kit to remove the cloth and place it in an evidence bag.

Had Snickers tried to get a piece of the thief? Had the thief grabbed for Snickers? No wonder her poor cat was so shaken. *Attack cat.* Maggie shook her head at the thought.

Try as she might to avoid it, her mind kept returning to the letter and James's sudden disappearance from church.

That's crazy.

He had seemed genuinely upset that she had entered the house before he had a chance to check it out. And he seemed not to know anything about the trunk or what it had been hiding.

It was time to separate fact from suspicion.

She knew that the trunk had belonged to the Bennetts, at least for a time. She wasn't yet sure how his grandmother had gotten it. And she had no idea who had written that letter or who had been the intended recipient.

She didn't have the opportunity to examine the cloth Snickers had snagged, but the color looked suspiciously like James's shirt. Was his blazer hiding a tear?

James had made a point to tell her he took a walk outside the church. She had no idea when he had returned. Pastor David and the choir members were the only ones in a position to see the comings and goings of the congregation. *Dare I ask one of them?*

Again, she tried to shove the ugly thought from her mind, but it persisted. James knew where she kept the letter. She had told him the night before, after dinner. He could have had enough time to get to the manor and make it back to the church before the choir finished their last verse.

No, not James.

Maggie tried to treat Monday morning like any other day, but she couldn't stop thinking about the break-in and attempted burglary. She refused to accept that anyone she saw daily, knew from church, did business with, or cared about would try to crack open her safe.

To take her mind off of it, she busied herself with lists for Thanksgiving shopping and party preparations, despite the fact that everyone she'd told about her open house so far had declined the invitation. But she was still hopeful. There were plenty of other folks who could be getting their mailed invitations at that moment and were deciding to break from tradition and stop by Sedgwick Manor.

As she walked through the library to the office, she caught Captain Sedgwick's eye. "What happened here yesterday?" She stopped in front of the portrait and stood with her hands on her hips. "Is someone after that letter?"

The captain seemed to think so.

Maybe the letter is valuable beyond measure. It could have historical significance.

She made a note to research famous bank robberies in New York in 1930. Maybe the note was connected to a well-known event.

Maggie also had to consider that the break-in wasn't about the letter at all but simply about money or valuables. Perhaps the intruder had been scared off before he got anything. The old manor did produce a lot of startling creaks and groans. They still occasionally set her on edge.

This house needs some activity.

Maggie's mind went to Emily, who'd always kept the cottage in Bennington lively with friends and music and chatter. On a whim, she emailed her daughter and informed her of the new plans she'd made for Thanksgiving at Sedgwick Manor. She suggested that Emily bring any of her classmates who were stuck in the same boat with her, "if you get caught up on all of your work and need a break." Having people her own age to socialize with might entice her daughter to spare a few hours for the holiday.

When the lights went on in the Carriage House, Maggie dressed and walked over. Her breath made foggy clouds as she scuttled over the footbridge. The stream had a tissue-thin layer of ice. Even though the shop was officially closed on Mondays, Maggie now expected to find June there, using the time to do paperwork and hold private consultations.

June offered a melodic good morning to Maggie as she burst through the door.

"It's my first Thanksgiving here, and I want to make it memorable." Maggie handed an invitation to June. "Would you like to come to my open house?"

"Oh, I'm sorry, but we're going to spend the day with my parents and sisters inland. It's our tradition, and then they come here for Christmas, when both of our girls are with us."

"That sounds like fun." Maggie engaged in some cheerful small talk about June's family traditions before she went back in the workshop to fuss with the trunk.

As she sanded, she thought about the original owners, how they must have struggled, and what they did when they couldn't be together. It struck Maggie that she had so much in her life.

So what if things aren't going as planned? If she wanted to prepare a feast, she would prepare a feast. If no one showed up, she'd freeze it and have homemade turkey dinners all winter.

It'll be the year of Thanksgiving leftovers.

· · · · · · · · · · · · · · · · · ·

That afternoon, Nate showed up to trim trees and replace her locks. Maggie hadn't expected him to get the specialty hardware so quickly, but one of the guys on Nate's crew was in Portland over the weekend, so he picked them up from the distributor.

Filled with gratitude, she tried to give Nate a tip to reward his employee, but he refused it. "It really wasn't a problem."

Then she forced it on him by teasing that she would hover around, asking questions while he worked, until he took it. "I like answering questions," Nate said, but he took the money and slipped it into his pocket.

Maggie was comforted to know she was now the only person with a key to Sedgwick Manor. She thought of the irony of it—installing new locks while hoping her house would get invaded come Thanksgiving Day.

She was regretting that she'd asked for RSVPs. That was no way to host an open house. She made a few phone calls to people who had declined to let them know that even if they had other plans, they should still feel welcome to drop in.

Satisfied that she'd remedied her social faux pas, Maggie decided to do some research at the library. Armed with photos of the vaudeville decals and the name Schuler, she left her sleeping cat and stepped outside.

Storm clouds formed in the distance. A few waterspouts danced like whirling dervishes over the surface of the dark gray water. *Not another storm.*

On her way through town, she stopped in at Fran's shop to see if the quilt she wanted was still there. She'd had so much going on, she'd forgotten about it until she was walking past The Quilt Cupboard.

At thirty-six, Fran was the youngest owner among the artisan shops in town. With her dark hair pulled back in a ponytail, slender form, and pale, flawless skin, she looked even younger.

Unfortunately, Fran had already sold the peony-patterned quilt. She showed Maggie a few others, but she wasn't captured by them like she had been by the one Deborah Bennett had made. Naturally, she asked about James's mother, but all Fran said was "She's a lovely person." Maggie didn't press for more.

In the library, Maggie was headed for the history books when that shelf of Somerset Harbor High School yearbooks beckoned to her again. She detoured toward them and scanned the spines. Deborah Bennett, née Keene, was likely about the same age as Aunt Evelyn, perhaps a few years younger.

Without too much searching, she found Deborah Keene's photo, which showed an attractive blond-haired, doe-eyed girl with an aura of sadness about her. Her photo stood out in those rows upon rows of smiling students. Maggie imagined a frustrated photographer trying to coax a smile onto that pretty face.

It seemed that whatever had happened to make Deborah's life miserable had happened well before this photo was taken. In contrast to most of the other students, she listed no organizations or clubs or interests. *Had she been reclusive even at that young age?*

Suddenly, inspiration struck. Maggie returned the yearbook to its shelf and raced home. She pulled out her favorite stationery and wrote a note:

> *Dear Mrs. Bennett,*
>
> *My name is Maggie Watson. Evelyn Bradbury was my aunt, and she left me Sedgwick Manor and Carriage House Antiques when she passed away earlier this year. Your son has gone out of his way to make sure I feel welcome here and has become a friend of mine.*

I'm writing because I saw one of your beautiful quilts, the one decorated with peonies, at The Quilt Cupboard and fell in love with it. But someone else purchased it before I could. I would like to commission a similar quilt. If I don't hear to the contrary, I will plan to stop by at nine this coming Wednesday morning to discuss it. I look forward to meeting you.

She called Ruth and got Deborah's address, then rushed out to hand-deliver her note. Maggie had included her phone number, so if Deborah didn't want her to visit, she could call.

One way or another, she hoped she would get to talk to Deborah Bennett.

. . . .

Maggie filled the day before she was to see James's mother by busying about the house and seeking out, washing, and assembling things she would need for her party. Even though it was still over two weeks away, she spread the buffet with a tablecloth, fanned out napkins, set up chafing dishes, and stacked plates.

Preparing for a big event at Sedgwick Manor was easier than she'd anticipated. She'd never have been able to manage setting up this far in advance at her Bennington cottage. But in her spacious new home, she could put things out without disrupting her own daily routine.

She realized at one point during the day that she was bracing for her cell phone to ring, with Deborah Bennett on the other end scolding Maggie for inviting herself over. *Honestly, what were you thinking?* But the call never came.

On Wednesday, Maggie stopped at the grocer's and picked up a pot of bright yellow mums. Standing on the front stoop of Deborah Bennett's white clapboard home, she shifted from foot to foot, feeling anxious. She had considered that James's reclusive mother might simply leave her to stand outside. The woman had no obligation to open her home to a pushy newcomer.

Poised to set the plant on the porch and leave, Maggie was surprised when the door opened.

Deborah was dressed in a dark blue crepe dress with a hand-crocheted collar and matching cuffs. Her honey-color hair was laced with gray and was gathered into a neat bun. She wore no makeup on her porcelain skin. "Ms. Watson? Come in."

"Call me Maggie, please. Thank you for seeing me."

"Curiosity got the better of me, I must admit. My son has mentioned you a number of times. And of course, someone who appreciates my quilt designs is of interest to me." She motioned to a Queen Anne wing chair in gold brocade.

A teapot with a sprinkling of violets sat between them on a serving table. Maggie recognized the design as Royal Albert bone china. She had a box of six teacups and saucers with that very design in the shop's storage. There had been a note on it in Aunt Evelyn's handwriting: *Hold.*

The plain white cups that accompanied Deborah's teapot appeared to be of cheap glass. Maggie glanced around and saw a hurricane lamp identical to the one she'd brought from Vermont to complement its mate in Emily's bedroom at the manor. She wondered if all three had once graced this home.

The two chatted like old friends over tea and traditional Maine treats. "Needhams, the ones with the coconut, are from my childhood. And the whoopie pies are James's favorites."

Maggie couldn't decide which she liked more.

Talk eventually turned to Deborah's quilting skills. "I never make the same design twice." But she was inspired by the beautiful flowers Maggie brought and agreed to make a chrysanthemum quilt in graduating shades of yellow for Emily's room.

Deborah might have been reclusive, but she wasn't particularly guarded. She told Maggie that her Aunt Drusilla had helped raise her. "She was distrustful of everyone and stricter than most, I suppose. I grew up being comfortable in solitude. I lost my husband a few years after James was born, but I'm so glad he inherited his outgoing genes."

Deborah looked up at the sound of the back door opening and closing. "That would be my son with groceries for the week."

"Then I'd better go." Maggie set down the teacup. "I enjoyed myself, and I look forward to seeing that quilt." She stood.

James walked in and stopped short. "Maggie? What are you doing here?" He didn't sound happy to see her. The glower on his face seconded that.

"I . . ." Maggie suddenly felt like a sneak.

"That's no way to speak to a friend and guest." Deborah's tone was both surprised and scolding.

"Thank you for your hospitality," Maggie said pointedly to Deborah. "The treats were wonderful."

"And thank you for the flowers."

"I'll let you two visit." Maggie directed this comment to James. "And don't worry, I didn't eat all of the whoopie pies."

He didn't reply, but continued to frown at her.

Deborah shot her son the kind of look only a disappointed mother could conjure.

"Nice to see you," he said.

Maggie wanted to shrink into a dust mote and blow away. She pressed her lips together tightly as she looked him square in the eyes. She realized her presence was unexpected, but he looked more angry than shocked.

What's he so upset about? He should be glad that his mother isn't as reclusive as he thought.

She nodded in James's direction before walking with Deborah to the door.

The air was chilly and moist, with the taste of sea salt. Maggie slid behind the wheel of her Jetta and adjusted the rearview mirror. When she caught a glimpse of herself, she didn't like the gloom she saw.

She felt terrible that she'd caught James off guard. After showing him the purchase proof on the trunk, he probably thought she was there coaxing family skeletons from the closet to satisfy her own curiosity. *But James should trust me more.* Then again, she suspected him of breaking into her home, so she wasn't exactly trusting either.

She reassured herself that it was natural for her to wonder about the Bennett family, particularly since Deborah and her son were so different. Was James's smile and easy way with people bravado? Could it be that he worked hard to be accepted? It must've been difficult, returning to Somerset Harbor after he'd graduated college, with his fiancée's death hanging over him. He'd probably returned to help his mother.

She imagined him questioning his mother about their visit, worried that Maggie had broached forbidden subjects.

And I might have if I'd thought Deborah could have handled it, she thought guiltily.

She decided to invite Deborah to Thanksgiving even though James had already said that he and his mother had plans together. After all, Deborah had welcomed Maggie into her home and had been a gracious hostess.

On her way to Sedgwick Manor, she got backed up behind some cars on Shoreline Drive. *Peculiar.* There wasn't usually so much traffic in the small town.

As she tried to see what was happening, a figure materialized near her window, causing her to flinch. He shoved a card under her windshield wiper and winked at her. It was that dreadful DA candidate again—Davidson. She glared at him before pulling away.

When Maggie neared the manor, she looked down at the Carriage House parking lot and saw that the few cars there had political fliers under their windshield wipers too. Davidson was as persistent as a gnat and equally as annoying.

But there was too much to do over the next week to fret over him. He wasn't the real cause of her irritation anyway. A lot of things had her on edge: her house had been broken into, James was probably angry with her, and her Thanksgiving party was shaping up to be a mistake. After locking herself into Sedgwick Manor, she had to admit that the break-in was the primary contributing factor to her current stress level.

Maggie knelt in the hallway to give Snickers a scratch behind the ears. "It's good to see that you're on guard duty."

He bolted away from her when her phone rang. "Very brave," she said as she looked at the caller ID. It was her realtor in Bennington.

"You have a solid offer that's only a little under the asking price. It's from Professor Roland at the college. He and his wife fell in love with your house. I think this is probably the best offer you'll get."

The name was familiar. Professor Roland was in the English department and would probably be dean when the current dean retired. They were a young couple; the house would be perfect for them.

"Accept it. Do I need to return to sign the papers, or can it be handled from here?"

"I'll overnight the paperwork to you when it's ready. All you have to do is get your signature notarized. And Maggie, congratulations."

When they hung up, she was surprised by how little nostalgia she felt. Sedgwick Manor was home now, and there was nothing to gain by looking back. She would turn this giant manor into a home every bit as cozy as the cottage in Bennington had been. Still, it was a big change, and a permanent one.

She picked up Snickers, who had returned to the hallway to prance around as she talked on the phone. Maggie gave him a hug, partly in celebration, partly to comfort herself. The portrait of the captain peered out from the library.

Is that a twinkle in his eye?

Soon she'd put out the hand-blown ornaments and garlands she'd found in the attic. That would cozy the place up.

"This is going to be a wonderful Thanksgiving, even if you and I are the only two here." *Not that Snickers would care about that.*

She sincerely hoped that they wouldn't be. "It's hard being the new kid in town."

Snickers nuzzled her neck, then squirmed to get down.

"Okay, I guess we're done cuddling."

He bounded toward the front door and started pawing at a piece of paper that was on the floor. *Probably another political ad.* Maggie picked it up.

She stared at the bold, red block lettering, a waterfall of fear washing over her.

It read, *Back off, Ms. Watson.*

12

Maggie stared at the words. *Back off?* She could feel her blood pressure leap a few points. She was mildly pleased to note that she now felt anger, not fear.

How dare someone threaten me in my own home?

Was it a warning to stop her research? Who could possibly care besides James, or maybe some descendant of Schuler's? Or if it was a valuable piece, who knew? It could be a collector trying to scare her into getting rid of the letter before she found out its value.

She reluctantly called Officer Linton, who insisted on coming over to take a report and secure the evidence.

By the time he got there, Maggie had only gotten angrier. "I refuse to be intimidated." She put her hands on her hips and stood firm. "It was pretty brash of someone to come to my home in broad daylight and shove a threatening note under the door."

"If it weren't for the break-ins, this would've been considered a prank," Officer Linton said. "But I have to assume that whoever wrote it is trying to scare you. Unfortunately, without more to go on, all I can do is add this to your file."

"My file?" She grinned wryly. "That thing must be bursting at the seams."

After escorting Officer Linton out, Maggie admired the replica doorknob and hardware Nate had installed. Beautiful and secure. They had made her feel safer. Yet someone still managed to invade her space. She shook her head in dismay.

"I'm going to find out who did this." Maggie scooped up Snickers. "And they're going to be sorry they ever messed with us."

Her cat seemed to agree.

Since she hadn't yet given out any new keys to the manor, Maggie decided to hang on to the extras for the time being. Instead, she would make sure she was home on days when the housecleaning crew came, at least for now. She trusted the people who took care of Sedgwick Manor, but it seemed wise not to leave anyone alone in her house.

Before heading down to the workshop, she had a light lunch. She'd overdone it on sweets at Deborah's house. A crisp fall apple, a chunk of cheddar, and a handful of walnuts would do. As she ate, she listened to her voice-mail messages. There were a few more regrets from friends who were spending the holiday with relatives. Maggie didn't let it bother her. Even if the turnout was sparse, she was sure it would still be a nice first Thanksgiving in Somerset Harbor.

Feeling guilty about leaving Snickers again, she tugged on her coat and went to give him a goodbye cuddle. She found him in the library, sleeping on the back of the settee. He barely opened an eye to acknowledge her. "I'll be back soon."

Snickers flicked the tip of his tail in her general direction.

"I guess I'm dismissed."

Stepping out into the cool fog, Maggie walked to the Carriage House. As she crossed the bridge over the stream, she noticed that the ice was more opaque. Was it possible that there would be snow by Thanksgiving?

She hadn't been in the workshop more than a few minutes when she got a call on her cell phone from Emily. She sounded rested and free of her cold.

Maggie took a deep breath. "An English professor and his wife are buying the cottage. I'll be signing the final papers as soon as their loan goes through."

After a long pause, Emily said, "I didn't think it would happen so quickly. It feels so . . . final."

"I suppose it's time for another family to live a happy life there." She felt wistful out of empathy for her daughter.

"When you put it like that, I guess it was meant to be." A resigned sigh came through from the other end of the line.

"Have you given any thought to coming for Thanksgiving and bringing some friends? It could be fun."

"No can do, Mom. If I want to pass these tests, I'm going to need all the study time I can get."

Maggie wished her daughter luck and gave her the usual advice about taking care of herself. It was a stressful time for Emily, and she felt awful for adding to it by telling the poor girl that she'd sold her childhood home.

After hanging up, Maggie returned to restoring the trunk, hoping a little hard work would clear her mind. She'd been at it for about an hour when she got up to stretch and look out the window.

In the low afternoon light, she was surprised to see James near the side door of the manor. *What's he up to?* After their cold interaction at his mother's, she didn't think she'd be seeing him so soon.

She pulled on her jacket, strode through the shop, and burst out the entrance—straight into James.

"Whoa!" he exclaimed, steadying her. "Where are you rushing off to?"

"I saw you through the window and wanted to catch you." *In the act.* She felt her cheeks warm.

"When I didn't find you at home, I figured you were here." He held out a small box. "It's an ornament someone brought in for restoration years ago, but they never came to claim it. Think of it as a housewarming gift."

"Thank you so much." Maggie opened the box and drew back the tissue to reveal a delicate glass angel with gossamer wings. "It is absolutely beautiful. It'll make a wonderful addition to my Christmas tree."

"I'm sorry for my reaction earlier. My mother doesn't ever entertain guests, so I was speechless when I saw you there."

"I admire the way you protect her. She's a lovely woman."

"She said the same thing about you."

"Then will you change your mind and bring her to Sedgwick Manor for Thanksgiving?"

"I'm afraid not. I'm amazed that she felt comfortable having you for tea. But you won't be alone. Has your daughter changed her mind?"

"No. She's still in the frenzy of finals." She sighed.

"I remember how that was," James said. "I didn't come home much when I was at school."

Maggie resisted the urge to press him on details from that time in his life, knowing it was shrouded under a cloud of grief. "It'll be an open house, so you're welcome to drop in if your plans change."

He thanked her and then turned to leave.

"Before you go, would you like to see the trunk? I think I've done a pretty good job on it, but I could use an expert's opinion." Maggie hoped that seeing it would evoke more than an opinion of her work. She thought he might offer a little insight this time.

James swallowed hard but nodded. "Lead the way."

She took him through the shop to the workroom. "There. What do you think?"

He ran his hand over the wood. "Nice job."

"In a way, it was a shame to remove the dents and scratches. Some of those may have been from your cowboy boots. I felt like I was erasing your childhood."

"I have no sentiment about this trunk. I don't know why, but I don't even like it." He backed away as he spoke. "Maybe the horse threw me once." Despite the joke, his voice was hollow.

Before she could ask any questions, he excused himself to speak to June, and he soon beat a hasty retreat from the workshop. She listened for sounds of their conversation but heard only a quick murmur. Then the bell over the front door signaled his departure.

Maggie ran her fingers over the sanded portion of the trunk. She could no longer feel any difference between it and the untouched area surrounding it. Satisfied she'd done all she could for the time being, she checked the wall clock in the workroom. The historical society was open until five, which meant she had enough time to swing by and see if Ruth could shed some light on the mysteries that plagued her.

Out in the showroom, June was putting lighted grapevine garland in the windows.

"It looks great," Maggie said. "Do you need help?"

"Thanks, but I've got a method to my madness. By Black Friday, this place will be transformed for Christmas."

"You know where to reach me." She waved her cell phone at June, hurried back to the manor, and jumped into her car.

The historical society was housed in an ornate Queen Anne Victorian. The pink-and-teal building stood out among the simple, clean lines of Somerset Harbor's white clapboard architecture. As Maggie approached the door, she spied a piece of paper attached to the frame. *More of Jeff Davidson's campaign fliers.* She yanked it down and stuffed it in her purse. *James would be proud of me.*

Inside, the house was precisely as it had been when acquired, though the dining room now had a podium and folding chairs for the members to conduct meetings. One wall was lined with framed photos of the families and individuals who meant something to the town. The adjacent room held filing cabinets and a table for research.

Not seeing Ruth, Maggie called out, "Hello?"

"I'm in here," Ruth Harper's voice rang out.

An avid needlework enthusiast, Ruth was at the kitchen table working on a project, her expression placid.

Maggie shed her coat, hung it across a kitchen chair, and sat.

"I was wondering if anyone would stop by before I closed up for the day." Ruth placed her embroidery project in tissue and set it aside. "I guess the ladies are getting ready for the holidays."

Maggie agreed, thinking how she might be panicking about her party if anyone had agreed to come.

"I'm brewing some jasmine tea." Ruth got up and walked to the teapot on the counter. "Would you care to join me?" She pulled out another mug from the cupboard without waiting for Maggie's answer.

"I took this off the front door." Maggie showed Ruth the offending flier. "Are you familiar with this Jeff Davidson?"

"Yes." Ruth placed the tea on the table, her face showing distaste for the man. "He's running for district attorney against Sam Skyler, who has my vote. Sam's a good man, around James Bennett and Robert Linton's age. He's currently the assistant DA and has been excellent for our town."

"Is Sam a native Harborite?"

"The Skylers have been here since the early or mid-twentieth century, I believe. They're a real success story. The first generations were fishermen who struggled to make a go of it. But then one of them ran off to the Big Apple during the Depression and made a name for himself—"

"In vaudeville?"

Ruth chuckled. "No, dear, in real estate. He returned a wealthy man and helped a lot of families keep their homes when times were tough. Sam is the first generation to go to law school and then into public service." Ruth picked up the teapot and asked Maggie if she wanted more.

"No thank you. But it really hit the spot. I just wanted to stop in to say hello." She carried her mug to the sink and washed it before leaving. "If it gets too lonely on slow days, give me a call. I'll bring a sampler to work on." She grabbed her coat. "Also, I know you sent your regrets for Thanksgiving, but if things change, please feel free to stop by."

"Thank you," Ruth replied. "I'm sure Sedgwick Manor must be lovely this time of year."

By the time Maggie got back home it was already dark outside. She gave Snickers a big hug and then checked his bowl and filled it with dry food. An unusual sound caught her attention. *That's not one I've heard before.* She froze and listened.

A definite rustling was coming from outside the kitchen window. Her heart jumped.

She turned off the light, then crept to the window and peered out. Sure enough, she glimpsed a dark figure hunched over by the house, a flashlight panning the bushes.

Somebody's out there!

Snickers picked up on Maggie's fear and switched his tail back and forth, on high alert with her.

Maggie was about to pull out her cell phone when the knocker clattered against her front door. She could have laughed in relief. *Prowlers don't knock.*

Standing on the front porch in the pool of light was her landscaper and handyman, Nate Gregory.

"You gave me a fright. What were you doing out there in the dark?"

"I'm sorry I scared you, Ms. Watson. Last time I was here, I noticed that you lost some bushes. I wanted to check how many I needed to replace." He clicked his flashlight on and pointed it at the ground by the house. "Given that you've had a break-in, I thought you ought to know there are some large footprints around the house. I'm sure they weren't there when I was last here."

Goose bumps crawled down her arms. "They don't belong to one of your crew?"

"My guys wear work boots. This was a different kind of tread. Sneakers, I'm guessing."

"I'll tell the police then." She was not looking forward to making that call. "Thanks for letting me know. By the way, I do feel much more secure with the new locks."

"I could install some motion lights for you." He pointed his flashlight to the top corner of the house.

"I think I'll pass, at least for now. We get a lot of wildlife around here. I'm afraid they'd be setting off the lights all night." She did not want to create new ways to feel jumpy in the manor.

When Nate left, Maggie went to her bedroom, slumped onto her bed, and pulled the quilt around her. It had been a long day. Snickers hopped onto her lap, and she absentmindedly stroked his fur as she tried to settle her concerns.

Eventually, she pulled out her cell phone and called Officer Linton to report the newest development. She wondered if the footprints outside her window would match the muddy print that had been left inside.

Now if the prints had come from loafers, she'd know exactly who it was. She remembered that Jeff Davidson had worn loafers. Thinking of him, in her mind's eye, she saw the campaign fliers he had placed on the cars of customers at the Carriage House. *Maybe he saw who was lurking outside my windows.*

Maggie scoffed, thinking of him pushing a political ad into the hand of a bewildered burglar. Then she deflated a bit. If she wanted to find out if he'd noticed someone in sneakers skulking around her place, she was going to have to actually have a conversation with Jeff Davidson. *Prepare to be called "young lady."*

Suddenly, she got an uneasy feeling accompanied by a hunch. Although the shop clientele hardly seemed like the type to break into homes, she wished she knew who June had told about the letter. It was dark and cold outside, and Maggie was tired and hungry, but she couldn't let it rest. She put on her coat, grabbed her flashlight, and plodded down the path to the Carriage House. She unlocked the door to the antiques shop and flicked on the light.

At the counter, she pulled out June's notebook with customer preferences and wish lists. She was glad to see that it was more organized than Aunt Evelyn's journal. Finding the tab marked *Ephemera*, she turned to that page.

Aside from James, the list contained the names Rutledge, Peters, Davidson, Wallis, and Skyler. She wrote them down in her notepad. Then Maggie returned June's journal to its proper place and locked up.

The clouds had covered the moon with a thick gray blanket. As she panned her flashlight up, the bare trees by the path looked as if they could reach out to snatch her. She hastened her pace, sending a nearby raccoon scurrying for cover.

Safely locked inside the manor, Maggie didn't dare give in to the comfort of her chair. She immediately put some water on the stove to boil spaghetti, pulled sauce out of the fridge, and sliced off a piece of sourdough bread. She didn't care if she overloaded on carbs for dinner; she was officially starving.

As she sat and looked at the list of names from June's journal, she was struck that Skyler and Davidson were both ephemera collectors. She wondered if that was a common interest among politicians. *First James, and now these two DA candidates?*

Maggie would look into all of the names on the list. Someone wanted that letter, and she intended to find out who it was.

13

Daylight was streaming through the window when Maggie sat bolt upright in bed, a sharp pain in her forearm. Groggy and confused, she soon realized that Snickers had his claws sunk into her skin. She pulled herself free and scolded her cat.

But he ignored her. He stared at the wall, claws still extended and ears pointed forward as he listened intently.

Then she heard it too. A scratching sound was coming from . . . *inside the wall?*

Maggie threw back the quilt, swung her feet off the bed, and slid them into her fuzzy slippers. She reached for her chenille robe and quickly wrapped herself in it.

She turned to Snickers. "If I'm not back in two minutes, dial 911."

Her sense of humor didn't help her one bit as she crept into the hall, listening intently. Her heart thumped against her ribs as she entered the library. She could hear the scratching from that side of the wall too. Maggie pounded the plaster with her fist and the noise stopped. But after a moment, it resumed.

Whatever it was, it was between the walls. Had someone discovered the listening room that she herself had never been able to find? More likely a small animal had found its way into the walls and was nesting for the winter.

She returned to the bedroom to report to Snickers. "Whatever it is, it isn't going to attack us and steal our letter."

Her cat didn't seem soothed by this.

Maggie hadn't slept well, and being abruptly awakened didn't help. But she had a mission. Today she would find out about those names on her list.

After a hot shower and a pep talk about how she was getting closer to finding out who broke into her house, she felt a little better. The frost on the lawn inspired her to dress in her coziest clothes—a pair of soft wool socks, flannel-lined khakis, and a light blue microfleece pullover.

"Move it, lazybones. I need to make the bed." As she tugged at the quilt to hurry Snickers off, she heard the sickening sound of fabric ripping. Her heart sunk. "Oh no!" She carefully lifted her treasured blanket to investigate. Sure enough, she saw a tear about four inches long on the quilt top.

She closed her eyes in regret. It was as if she'd hurt a friend.

Pull yourself together. It's a quilt. And luckily, there was an expert on them right down the road in Somerset Harbor.

On her way out to The Quilt Cupboard with her blanket bundled in a protective bag, she intercepted the cleaning crew unloading their supplies from their van. Maggie had forgotten they were coming. She let them into the house, lingered for a minute in the foyer, and then decided that if Aunt Evelyn had trusted them, so should she. She handed out a spare key and took off.

At The Quilt Cupboard, Fran smiled and then turned serious when she looked from the bundle to Maggie's face. "What's wrong?"

"My quilt ripped." Maggie heard the concern in her own voice. "My mother and grandmother made it. It's as old as I am. Please tell me it can be repaired."

Fran gently unfolded the blanket and laid it across one of the bed-size tables. "It's beautiful." She smoothed it out tenderly and examined the tear with a magnifying glass.

Maggie bit her lip, waiting for the verdict.

"It can be mended. A jagged tear is actually easier to repair than a straight cut. It won't be perfect, but it'll be a little story that you can tell your grandchildren someday." Fran patted the quilt as if it were an infant in need of comfort. "My favorite quilt has cough syrup and chocolate ice cream stains from when I had pneumonia as a child. But those stains tell the story of how my mom took care of me." Her face glowed as she talked about her precious quilt. "The imperfections and flaws become part of each quilt's charm."

"I'll try to see it that way."

"Reweaving is a slow, delicate process, but it won't show too badly. I'll have your beautiful quilt back to you as quickly as I can manage."

"Thank you. I can't tell you how much better that makes me feel."

"I understand. My childhood quilt is also an old friend."

Assured that her heirloom was in good hands, Maggie headed out into the frosty air to The Busy Bean.

Daisy had her hair swirled into something resembling a beehive atop her head, and she'd clipped a jeweled bumblebee to it, showing Daisy's flare for whimsy. But she frowned when she saw Maggie.

"Honey, what's wrong? You look like something the cat dragged in that the dog wouldn't have."

"I'm fine. I ripped my heirloom quilt this morning. But Fran thinks she can fix it."

"Well, cheer up. That's good news." Daisy waved her hand, dismissing Maggie's situation as temporary. "A cup of coffee'll make you walk tall."

"I'll have the mocha blend, please." Maggie felt exhaustion in every bone.

"I've got fruit-and-nut muffins fresh from the oven."

"That sounds delicious."

"Speaking of delicious," Daisy said, dropping her voice to a conspiratorial tone, "look who's here. Why it's Alderman Bennett, the cavalier bachelor."

Maggie couldn't help but smile. Daisy's exuberance was good medicine on a day that started out on the wrong foot.

James was barely out of breath though Maggie could see he'd been jogging.

"Daisy, that hairdo is definitely you." He gazed questioningly at Maggie. "Are you all right?"

Her shoulders sagged in defeat. "I'm wishing I could hit the restart button today."

"Want to talk about it?" He gestured to the vacant table by the window.

Maggie agreed, reminding herself of her quest. She was going to get a chance to ask James about some of the names on her list.

As he got his coffee and made small talk with the people in the café, it was clear that the people of Somerset Harbor truly respected him. They perked up in James's presence.

"So, what do you recommend for uninvited guests?" she asked when he joined her.

"Prowlers again?" His eyes widened.

"I don't think so. Unless prowlers like to get inside the walls and make a lot of scratching noises. It woke up the cat, who found a very dramatic way to wake me up." Maggie revealed the claw marks on her arm. "I thought someone had found the secret tunnels."

"Is that old myth still haunting you? The field mice were probably moving in for the winter. They're pretty harmless. Most folks move over a little and make room. But if they're bothersome, you could call Nate."

"I think I can share the manor with them for a bit." Maggie wasn't sure if Snickers would like it, but she didn't want to hurt them. "They're so cute. I've seen them skittering off with their cheeks full of corn when the birds aren't watching."

"Ah, you invited them in with promises of food."

Maggie nodded. "I guess I did. Who knows? They might discover those secret passageways you don't believe in."

"Y'all are talking about field mice?" Daisy sidled up to their table. "I read about some of those critters in Virginia carrying off an engraved spoon in the 1600s. A descendant of the original owner found it during renovations in the nineteenth century. It's how he was able to finally prove that he was a legitimate heir to some noble family in England. How about that?" She didn't wait for their response, but sashayed off to entertain at another table.

"She must have supersonic hearing," Maggie said.

"I heard that," Daisy called over her shoulder.

James laughed and then turned his attention back to the problem at hand. "If you wait until spring, they'll abandon their winter digs. Then you can figure out how they got in and close it up. And you shouldn't believe that gossip about secret passages and rooms. No one's ever found any evidence of it."

"That doesn't mean it isn't there." However, she often wondered if Aunt Evelyn had made up the story to entertain Maggie as a child. "But I see that you're far too practical to be convinced without hard evidence, which I will produce eventually." She pointed her fork at him and then took a bite of her muffin.

"Please don't start knocking holes in the walls to prove me wrong."

"Not while the mice are in there." She took a sip of her mocha and put her mug down with purpose. "As a full-fledged citizen of this town, I've been meaning to ask if you can take care of something for me."

"I'll do what I can."

"I've got a trash problem. Every time I venture out into Somerset Harbor, I get a Davidson flier shoved in my hand."

James shook his head. "Sam Skyler is the man to fix that."

"I haven't seen anything about him yet."

"Sam will campaign at the proper time. The election isn't until April." He glanced around at the other patrons and then leaned closer. "I suppose I'm not breaking Daisy's no-politics rule by saying that Davidson has amassed millions as a criminal defense attorney throughout New England. He became a landowner in town when he defended a local man who cost some here considerable savings through a Ponzi scheme.

"Even though he lost the case, Davidson got the guy's mansion and anything else that wasn't seized. Let's just say he's far from popular here. My guess is he's counting on his marriage to an admired widow, Lydia Rodgers, and the fact that he's playing stepfather to her son, to make him palatable to the voters. What else he has in mind I haven't a clue, but I can guess that it'll be sleazy. My take on him is that he'd do anything to win."

"Interesting." Maggie remembered the disdain on Ruth's face at the mention of the man. "Lydia, you say? I haven't met her yet."

"You've met her son, Jarrod."

"Jarrod who works with Bobby Linton? He's a nice kid."

"Despite having Davidson as a role model."

"Tell me about Skyler."

"Sam's down-to-earth and a good prosecutor. He's been an assistant DA for five years. He wants to be a good district attorney for us, while Davidson's agenda is probably to work his way up to state and then to national politics, and he'd probably like to skip a few steps. I've known Sam since high school. I trust him to do a good job." James stared out the window before speaking again. "He didn't have to, but he took me under his wing in high school and mentored me. He cracked a protective shell I'd built around myself and made me see that I could rise to my challenges."

"He sounds like a good friend."

James nodded.

"Ruth mentioned that the Skylers were wealthy. Did he earn it as a prosecutor?"

"You don't get rich as a government servant. As far as I know, the Skylers have had money for generations."

"He sounds interesting. I'd like to meet him." *Particularly since he's on the list of collectors June might have told about the letter.*

"That's right, you didn't meet Sam at church. He started coughing and left."

Maggie blinked. *James had seen Sam leave the sanctuary?* That meant James had come inside even before Pastor David began his sermon.

Relief washed over her. She didn't want to be suspicious of James, and now she didn't have to be.

But . . . Sam didn't return.

He would have had plenty of time to get to the manor while Maggie was at church. But why would he if he was such a fine man with plenty of money?

Maggie decided that while she tried to figure out a possible motive, she would continue to look at the other names on June's list of ephemera collectors. She didn't feel much closer to the truth, but this hadn't been a complete dead end.

At least James Bennett was officially off her list of suspects.

14

Maggie put on her jacket and stepped outside, inhaling the brisk morning air and releasing it with a satisfying "Ahhhh." Frost on the brittle grass reflected the sun like diamonds. She scurried to the mailbox, which held several envelopes. Eager to open the responses to her invitations, she snapped the box shut and dashed back into the house.

Soon the house would smell of cinnamon, brown sugar, and yeast. Thanksgiving was less than two weeks away, and she was planning on spending a few hours making dough to freeze for piecrusts, cookies, and bread. Maggie wanted to make the few days before the big event as relaxed and enjoyable as possible.

She spread the mail on the table and sat down to open it. Most were declines; a few said maybe. She disregarded the rejections, determined to forge ahead, as unflappable as Aunt Evelyn and Captain Sedgwick.

Surprised to see a handwritten envelope with Deborah's return address, she tore it open, finding an invitation to tea on Sunday to select the fabrics for her chrysanthemum quilt.

Maggie didn't want another situation like before, when James hadn't been expecting to see her, so she made a plan to run into him later that day. She would treat herself to lunch at The Busy Bean after all of her hard work baking. If she didn't run into him "by accident," she would go to his office.

Sure enough, James stopped by the café as Maggie was finishing the last of her chicken salad sandwich, and she told him about her plans to go to his mother's house on Sunday.

"Why don't I go with you? We can make a day of it. I'll take you to church. Then before we stop by my mother's, we can go to Nate's tree farm and reserve our trees."

Maggie was amused by the idea of picking out her Christmas tree in advance.

It seemed normal to James. "I like to get the pick of the crop."

"It sounds like fun, but you should know that I'm going to ask your mother about your awkward teen years."

"You'll be disappointed. I was always this charming." He leaned back in his chair and stretched his legs out, crossing them at the ankles.

"Are you charming?" Maggie asked with a tilt of her head.

"Very funny."

"I'll go to Nate's with you, but I've got a magnificent artificial tree. It's big and bright white with all of the decorations already on it."

James was briefly taken aback. "That sounds interesting," he managed to squeak out.

Maggie laughed. "I'm kidding. I'm more of a New England traditionalist. I really go all out for Christmas."

"Evelyn always did. She had a giant tree in the living room packed with ornaments. It was really unbelievable."

But Maggie could believe it since she'd inherited all of those decorations as well as the ones for Thanksgiving. She planned on putting them up that afternoon. She'd purposely saved the task as a special treat for herself.

When she got home, Maggie opened the boxes of hand-blown Thanksgiving ornaments. She studied each one before placing it on the mantel—corncobs, turkeys, pumpkins, blushing apples, and Pilgrims. On the table, she centered a cornucopia with ornamental squash spilling from it. She draped the garlands over the curtain rods and placed a wreath of miniature pumpkins, squash, and autumn leaves on the front door.

Standing back to admire her handiwork, she said to Snickers, "Our first Thanksgiving here is really shaping up."

He rubbed against her leg, purring in agreement.

. . . .

That Sunday at church, James ushered Maggie to the pew next to the Lintons, saying hello to several parishioners on the way. When they sat, he told her that Sam Skyler was sitting in the back of the church and he would introduce her to him later. She tried to catch a glimpse of the assistant DA, but she didn't know what he looked like.

Unfortunately, after the service, Sam was gone.

Using the feeble excuse that she had to check in on Snickers, Maggie asked James to drive her home. She rushed in to inspect her safe, but no one had broken in. She felt silly for jumping to conclusions. However, she considered that it was the new locks that had kept Sam out.

James drove them inland a few miles to Nate's tree farm, and Maggie was amazed to see how many people were there, tagging their trees. Birds shrilled and squirrels chattered a hoarse protest at the intruders. The two strolled along the rows of fragrant pines of every imaginable size.

"Perfect!" Maggie finally exclaimed. "I can definitely see this one with the beautiful angel you gave me on it." She attached her tag to a limb at eye level and inhaled the fresh scent.

James tagged a six-foot tree for his apartment, a slightly larger one for his office, and a five-foot one for his mother's home.

When they arrived at Deborah's, she greeted them with hugs. Maggie handed her a gift-wrapped cup and saucer that matched Deborah's teapot. Maggie had retrieved the items from the box in storage at the Carriage House. She had limited her gift to the single set so as not to embarrass Deborah by giving her a box of china that had probably been hers at one time. Deborah seemed genuinely pleased, and the visit proceeded pleasantly.

As James drove Maggie home, he was relaxed as he talked about his grandmother, Sally; his great-grandmother, Priscilla; and his great-aunt, Drusilla. "Aunt Drusilla helped Sally raise my mother after Priscilla died young. She was very strict and reclusive and didn't let my mother take part in school activities or anything outside the home. By the time I was born, Aunt Drusilla was ancient and terrifying." James pulled his car to a stop in front of the manor.

"Do you have time to come in?" Maggie asked. "You still haven't seen that letter I found."

"Right. I've been meaning to take a look."

"I have no idea if it's authentic or even truthful. I can't find much in Aunt Evelyn's journal. There was only the notation that said some stories are best left untold."

"It's a love letter, you say?"

"Not exactly."

"I'll be able to tell if the paper is authentic by the watermark. Whether or not it's valuable is another matter." James retrieved a pair of gloves from his car and followed Maggie.

Inside, he leaned over and ran his hand the length of Snickers's back. The tabby rolled over, squirming happily. While Maggie put coffee on to brew, James admired the Thanksgiving decorations.

After retrieving the envelope from the safe, she waited until James put on his gloves. Then she handed the letter to him.

"June and I have both handled it." Maggie looked pointedly at his gloved hands.

"As have many people, I'd imagine." He held the delicate paper lightly. "It's a professional habit." His brow furrowed as he read. "Bank robbery. I hardly know what to say."

Walking to the window, he held the paper to the light. A pale watermark of a monkey hanging from a tree appeared. "I recognize that mark. It's from the Avalon Paper Company, which went out of business around 1900. The last of the stationery probably disappeared from shops within the next few years."

Maggie stared over his shoulder at the watermark. "Fascinating."

"I'm astounded." He walked back to the table and sat. "You found this hidden in the lining of that trunk?"

"Yes, the very same trunk you played cowboy on as a toddler. Of course, your family might have acquired it after the letter was concealed there. Or it could have been tucked inside by Aunt Evelyn. Who knows?"

James shook his head. "I wasn't really privy to family secrets. It was always apparent that something pretty bad had happened in the past, and that was why the women lived like hermits." He tapped on the tabletop with a gloved finger. "Vaudeville musician caught up in a bank robbery? That's pretty scandalous."

"It was the Depression."

"Ever since this business with the trunk has come up, I've been remembering more from my childhood." James leaned back. "I found an old trumpet once. It might have even been from that trunk. I can still see Aunt Drusilla's twisted face as she snatched it from me."

"That's terrible." She could imagine that a trumpet blasting in a quiet house wasn't the most pleasant sound. But she used to pull her pots and pans from the cupboard to let Emily bang on them when she was a toddler, so it was safe to say Maggie had been fairly tolerant of high noise levels.

"Aunt Drusilla was a tyrant. I think the trunk was gone soon after that, but maybe it went to the attic, where I was forbidden to go." He tugged his gloves on a little tighter. "Do you really think I could have an accidental getaway driver in my family tree? Could that be why there's been so much secrecy?"

Maggie placed her hand on James's arm. "If you want to compare ancestors, my tree has a Viking who was called 'the Snake-Eyed' and a few moonshine runners on my dad's side."

He gave her a wan smile.

"We aren't responsible for our ancestors," Maggie continued. "Sometimes we can't even control circumstances here and now." She was thinking about his fiancée, Natalie Boarder, although she would never bring it up. She squeezed his arm and then withdrew her hand.

"No wonder my mother is so charmed by you." James grinned and turned his attention back to the letter. He studied it more closely this time. "Have you learned any more about this?"

Maggie shook her head. "I picked up a book on vaudeville, but it didn't mention any of The Palace entertainers turning to bank robbery. I did find out that it opened in 1913, but I have no idea how long the letter writer had been there before 1930. He must have been good because 'playing The Palace' was the most coveted job in the business. Some of the earliest film stars got their start there." Maggie ticked the names off on her fingers. "Bob Hope, Lillian Russell, Rudolph Valentino. When things started to decline, some of the musicians remained to accompany the silent movies, but all that was over by the early thirties." Maggie glanced out at the copse of pine trees, their boughs waving to her in the blue light of dusk.

"Let's say the trumpet I found was from the vaudeville trunk. That would mean whoever wrote this must have returned as promised."

"I don't know. Maybe it was shipped by train." Maggie had read that was a common practice.

James sighed. "I want to ask my mother, but I doubt she'd know. Nobody asked questions as long as Drusilla was alive." He put the letter back in the envelope.

"I don't want you to upset her." Maggie was getting a picture of the sad, lonely life Deborah Bennett had lived, and she couldn't imagine adding to her pain.

"Drusilla laid down the law, Sally enforced it, and my mother toed the line. Even after Drusilla died, her influence remained." James took off his gloves and tucked them into his pocket.

What a terribly oppressive environment. "Your father is deceased, isn't he?"

He nodded. "I barely remember him. He died before I started school."

As curious as she was about what made her friend the man he was, Maggie felt it was unfair to continue asking questions about his ancestors. The sun had set, and the room had darkened. "Will you stay for supper?" She had planned on reheating one of her freezer meals, but she would be able to whip up a nice pesto pasta if James wanted to stay.

"Thanks, but I'd better go. I have some invoices to handle. I want to get a jump on the week." He rose and replaced his chair. "Can I have a rain check?"

"Of course. It was a wonderful day. Thank you."

James started toward the door. "If you want to research my family history, I can call Ruth and tell her . . ." His voice trailed off, but he turned to look at her. "I'm curious, but I don't have the stomach to do it myself."

"I'll be sure to share what I learn, but only with you."

After she closed and locked the front door, Maggie leaned against it, her hand still on the doorknob. She let her breath out slowly.

Snickers trotted up and sat at her feet, watching her with big eyes. She scooped him into her arms and rubbed his fur with her chin. "I know, fuzzy one. You want your supper, don't you?"

In the kitchen, she opened a small can of cat food and then heated up her own dinner.

She'd missed her normal Sunday phone call with Emily but had gotten a short email from her. Things were still hectic for her cherished girl. Maggie replied by telling her to hang in there. "Keep yourself healthy and you'll get through this semester with flying colors."

As Maggie ate, she paged through her book about vaudeville. In its heyday, silent motion pictures were used to entertain audiences between live acts. Then new technology took over. By 1927, film and vaudeville roles were reversed.

She learned that most performers remained in one venue only a week before traveling by train to the next one. However, some musicians remained in one place. Maybe the trumpet player who'd written the letter had been a permanent orchestra member. If so, he might be in the city census records.

There were boardinghouses in New York City that catered especially to actors, entertainers, and musicians, who were transient tenants. She would look into occupancy records, if such a thing existed.

Maggie grabbed her notebook and added it to the list of things to research. She also left herself a reminder to search online for playbills from The Palace from 1927 through 1932. If she couldn't find any, she would see if June could find one for her.

Returning to her book, she learned that Bert Lahr and Ray Bolger—the Cowardly Lion and the Scarecrow in *The Wizard of Oz*—got their starts in vaudeville. Even Helen Keller, deaf and blind from a childhood illness, once had an act with her teacher and friend Anne Sullivan. Until she demonstrated her intelligence and humor to audiences, people with hearing impairments were often put into asylums. Vaudeville helped change that.

It's this legacy and the darling picture of the little cowboy that should be the humpback trunk's story, not the unanswered questions about desperate times and hardship.

She tried to imagine what life had been like for the author of the mysterious letter. The story began with joy, music, and talented entertainers. It ended with the slow descent into the same Depression that gripped the nation.

Aunt Evelyn was probably right when she said that there are some stories that were best left untold. That trunk was a Pandora's box that she wished she'd never opened.

She put it out of her mind until she was drifting off to sleep that night.

The trumpet, the trunk, the vaudeville stickers, the robbery, the letter—they all swirled together and pointed straight at James's family.

15

The next day, Maggie donned her peacoat and, on a whim, put on a 1950s gray felt hat with a matching feather she found in the storage room. When she opened the front door, the air smelled like wet mittens. She was thrilled by the possibility of snow, at least a light dusting to cover the dry, dead grass.

Although she normally enjoyed hitting the town on foot, she had a lot to do, so she took the Jetta. From Shoreline Drive, she could see that the ocean was dark and choppy. Tiny gray silhouettes of fishing and lobster boats bobbed beyond the breakwater. It must have been about time for shore duties like repairing nets and boats.

Maggie pulled into the parking lot next to The Busy Bean, thinking she needed to fortify herself for a long day of research. The warmth inside had caused the windows to fog up. Beads of moisture made erratic trails that crisscrossed into spiderweb designs.

Daisy was at the counter, pouring a mug of coffee for a customer and laughing heartily at something he'd said. Nearly every table and counter seat was occupied. There was nothing like the smell of snow in the air to draw people into a cozy café.

Maggie took the one seat open at the counter.

"Nice hat, honey," Daisy said.

"Thanks. I thought this would be a good day to try something different."

"Then my pumpkin spice brew is just the thing."

Maggie agreed. "To go, please."

Daisy's bean grinder sounded briefly, and in a few minutes she brought a fresh-brewed to-go cup that smelled spicy and strong.

Maggie took a sip and closed her eyes, savoring the taste. "My favorite so far."

Daisy grinned. "What are you up to today?"

"I'm brushing up on the history of my new town." It wasn't exactly a lie. "I'm off to see Ruth Harper."

"I can't think of a better person to help with that," Daisy told her. "Good luck, and bundle up out there."

As she approached the historical society, she smiled at the sight of the pink Queen Anne. *Maybe it's blushing from all the secrets it holds.*

Inside, Ruth greeted her warmly. "I got James's message that you're doing some research for him. I'm afraid that we don't have much on his people, although a good number of longtime Harborites have given us their family trees."

"Really?"

"A few years ago for Founders Day we encouraged people to submit their family histories. We got a big response." Ruth looked proud of the fact.

"I hope they went deeper than grandparents."

"We don't encourage people to include family members who are still living." Ruth opened a filing cabinet. "It makes it too easy for thieves to get a mother's maiden name."

"Why would they want that?"

"It's the most common question financial institutions use to verify your identity."

"Good point." Maggie hadn't considered how flimsy that security question was. She flipped her notepad open. "I've got some of James's family names already."

"Then you might want to start with the local cemetery records. Daisy has dedicated hours and hours of time to recording the tombstones." Ruth pulled out a folder and put it on the table. "We're also duplicating the church records of births, marriages, and burials, and we're collecting copies of family Bible listings." She showed Maggie where she could find those files. "We record wills when we can and court records."

"Those are great ideas, Ruth. Thanks." Although Maggie had been a history major in college, her research skills were rusty.

"If you have any problems with it, give me a holler." Ruth paused and gave Maggie a kind look. "It's so good to have as many active members as we can get, especially you young ones."

Maggie grinned. She hadn't thought of herself as one of the "young ones" in years.

As she rummaged through the folders, she wondered if her aunt had gotten this far or had only suspected as much as Maggie did now.

She searched the records from Old Faith Church and found that a Robert Keene and Sally Allen—James's grandparents—married soon after the end of World War II. Deborah's christening was listed in the church records, and Robert Keene's funeral was a year later.

A search of the tombstone records turned up a Priscilla Allen, age twenty-four. Sally must have been no more than a toddler when her mother died.

Sally Allen could be the infant mentioned in the secret letter. If so, was her father the vaudeville musician?

Maggie rubbed her eyes wearily.

She went through the tombstone records again, but found no other Allens. If the letter writer had been an Allen, he had not returned to Somerset Harbor.

"Daisy said you'd be here."

Maggie was so deep into the research that she hadn't even heard James come in. She stretched as she greeted him.

"I'm anxious to see if you've found anything. I would have stopped by earlier, but the drapery company delivered the wrong curtains to my client. It took a phone call to get it straightened out, but the woman was near hysteria. She wants everything perfect for Thanksgiving."

"Amateur." Maggie gave a dismissive wave. "That's over a week away."

James pulled up a chair and leaned over the papers that were spread across the table.

"I've found your grandfather Robert Keene, your grandmother Sally Allen, and her mother Priscilla, but nothing about Priscilla's husband. He might be our musician."

James nodded.

"Do you know his first name?" Maggie knew the answer to this before the question was even out of her mouth.

"No. I never asked."

"I suspect there's no way to ask your mother without upsetting her."

"Not that I can think of. And I definitely don't want to dredge up those memories for her. Grandmother and Great-Aunt Drusilla were furious when my mother used Allen for my middle name."

"Do you think your great-grandfather's first name was James?"

"I'm pretty sure it wasn't or I would have been called 'hey you' in the house."

Maggie was glad her friend still had his sense of humor. It was probably what saved him, growing up the way he did. "The trunk and the letter are the few pieces of evidence we have to work with, and they're not talking."

"That's not exactly true. That letter did some talking."

"You're right." Maggie sat up a little straighter. "And between the lines it said its writer wouldn't have willingly deserted his family. So there has to be another answer." She felt pretty sure the answer had something to do with Schuler.

"You think we're on the right track here? Could it be that my grandmother Sally is the infant that is referred to in the letter?"

Maggie rustled papers until she found the church christening. "The dates match. Sally B. Allen. Christened November 6, 1930."

Ruth stuck her head out of the kitchen. "Would either of you like some tea?"

Maggie looked up. "That sounds perfect right now."

"Thanks, but I have an appointment." James glanced at his watch. "Sorry for such a quick stop. I really appreciate you doing this for me."

"No problem." She was enjoying herself. Sure, it was frustrating at times, but it had lit a fire in her and reminded her why she loved history.

After James left, Ruth entered with a serving tray. "I've got tea and muffins. I hope you've had some luck. Anytime we can find an ancestor that has successfully hidden for decades, it's a victory."

"I feel the same way." Maggie took the tea Ruth handed her. "When I connected some of these dots today, it was a thrill."

A twinkle came to Ruth's eye. "Well then, let's have a celebratory muffin." Ruth handed Maggie a small china plate and pushed the pastry box closer.

Maggie hesitated.

"Don't leave me here with a dozen of Daisy's muffins."

"I'd never do that to you," Maggie joked.

Over tea, Ruth shared stories about researching triumphs and historical sleuthing. Maggie saw that they were kindred spirits. It wasn't everyone who could talk about digging through musty files with such passion. It amazed her to think that the life her aunt had built in Somerset Harbor had been so easy for Maggie to slip into.

She left the historical society feeling exhausted but exhilarated. She couldn't stop thinking about the letter, so full of love and hope. How could that man simply vanish without a trace?

She had the feeling she was closing in on getting the whole picture, and it wasn't going to be pretty.

As she got into her Jetta and turned over the engine, she saw something white wedged under her windshield wiper. *Probably another Davidson flier.*

She reached out and grabbed it. But it was not a political ad. It was a plain piece of paper with one word typed on it.

Stop.

16

Maggie added the threatening letter to her file at the police department and tried to carry on as usual. But in the quiet moments of the day when danger signs flashed across her mind, the first thing she felt was gratitude that Emily wasn't coming to Sedgwick Manor for Thanksgiving. She could picture herself constantly hovering and warning her daughter to stay safe, and that would make Somerset Harbor the last place she would ever want to visit again.

The next few days flew by, with research in the mornings and work at the antiques shop in the afternoons to help June get ready for the Black Friday rush. Together, they designed some new vignettes. Maggie's favorite had primitive kitchenalia, including carved wooden dough bowls, a butcher block, and collections of butter stamps, copper pots, and cast-iron pieces.

They decorated a game-room vignette with wooden cribbage, checkers, and backgammon boards. Its central focus was a marble tabletop chess board with carved alabaster pieces flanked by two tufted-leather wingback chairs. They filled weathered barn-wood shelves with old dice, handmade dominos, ornate mahjong tiles, and collectible playing cards. Then they added vintage signs, a basket of boccie balls, handsome wooden croquet sets, rackets, and bowls of marbles.

While June helped customers, Maggie changed the look of a sitting-room vignette by taking all of the nautical items that were scattered around the shop and grouping them together—a ship's figurehead, lobster traps, a freestanding brass steering wheel, and sailor folk art.

They saved a space at the very front of the store for their New England winter wonderland decor that June had staged in the workshop. She filled a sleigh with carved Santas, steel-runner sleds, wooden reindeer, and a feather tree covered in antique ornaments. "The day before Thanksgiving, I'll pull this out, set it up by the door, replace the pumpkins with poinsettias, and we're ready for Christmas."

There was a method to her madness.

The work was satisfying and allowed Maggie to mull over her research. The best working theory she had was that the trunk had belonged to Deborah's grandfather, a musician who worked in vaudeville. So, what had happened to him? If the letter contained so terrible a secret, why not destroy it? Had it been saved for blackmail? Was the mysterious Mr. Schuler involved? *Or maybe it's a Miss Schuler.*

As Maggie was adding this possibility to her notebook, she flipped to her to-do list. She still had some things she needed to accomplish before her open house, which was less than a week away. She left the Carriage House, intending to go to the grocery store, but found herself pulling into The Busy Bean parking lot. As she stepped inside, the bell announced her presence to an empty room.

Daisy came out of the kitchen, wiping her hands on a striped dish towel. "What a nice surprise. I don't usually see you with the after-work crowd."

Maggie looked around the empty café.

"They're coming." Daisy waggled her finger. "Make no mistake. This place will be packed soon enough. You early birds don't know the half of what goes on around here."

"Well, I intend to find out with the help of your pumpkin spice blend."

"That's yesterday's news." Daisy put her hand on her hip and shook her head. "This week it's all about salted caramel."

Maggie feigned disappointment.

"Always trust your barista." Daisy ignored Maggie's silent protest and filled a mug. "How about a table? I want to get off my feet for a minute."

They settled down by the window, both with big sighs.

"Long day?" Daisy asked.

"I was at the Carriage House all afternoon after spending the morning at the historical society. That tombstone information you recorded was such a big help."

Daisy fanned herself with her hand in spite of the cold outside. "I'm so glad to hear that. I tromped through the weeds and chiggers for weeks with my notebook. By the time I had them all, I was too tuckered out to alphabetize them." Daisy leaned in. "Honestly, I didn't know how to handle all of the spelling discrepancies and changes. Waggoner became Varner, MacQuarry became McCrary, Schuler became Skyler, and the Schneiders became, of all things, Taylors." She waved her hand dismissively. "You Yankees."

Maggie sat up, suddenly alert. "What did you say about Schuler?"

"Schuler became Skyler."

Daisy continued on about how Southerners all knew their roots by heart, but Maggie only partially listened as her thoughts shifted into overdrive. *Schuler changed his name!* He had returned to Somerset Harbor as a rich man called Skyler. Her heart began to pound.

I knew it! Sam Skyler. That's my man.

He knew about the letter. As a candidate for district attorney, he had a motive for stealing it to avoid a scandal about the source of his wealth. And she couldn't ignore that he'd had the opportunity to break into her house after ducking out of church with a supposed coughing fit.

All of this over something an ancestor did?

She wondered if his history would poison public opinion, or if Sam Skyler had simply gone overboard to protect his reputation.

Daisy's hearty laugh brought Maggie back to the conversation. "It took me years living up here to stop asking folks, 'Who are your people?' when I first met them. That's part of life down South. Chances are we could be cousins fifteen times removed or something. When I married Harry, I wanted to learn the history of the town and the people here. He couldn't go past his grandpa until I shook that family tree. Of course, whenever you shake a tree, a few nuts will fall out."

Maggie laughed. "Did you find much information about the Great Depression in these parts?"

Daisy cocked her head. "Are you looking for something in particular?"

"Not really." Maggie took a sip of her coffee. "I'm trying to get a general sense of how people weathered it here."

"It must've been pretty rough. Harry said folks ate what they could catch, grow, or barter until the country got back on its feet, so they survived. Those who were better off sold their valuables in the big cities where the wealthy could still afford to buy."

After Maggie drank her coffee and the café started filling up, she ordered a bowl of loaded baked-potato soup and a chopped salad to go for her dinner. She was finding she liked The Busy Bean's cooking as much as her own.

On the way home, Maggie considered what she'd learned. She needed to back up and rethink how the name change affected her whole theory.

The bank robber Schuler probably returned as the entrepreneur Skyler who had so generously saved the homes of Somerset Harborites when times were tough, including the home where

Deborah lived, she reasoned. A heavy conscience may have caused him to come through for the letter writer.

James had no idea how entwined his family and Sam's actually were.

. . . .

Maggie had anticipated getting home after dark, so she'd left the light on in the foyer. It nearly took her breath away as she turned up the drive. What an incredible sight that chandelier was. She wondered if Abigail Sedgwick had kept it on to welcome the captain home from the sea.

Inside, Snickers had planted his well-fed body in the center of the hall, facing the door. She was positive that if he could have tapped his foot with impatience, he would have. He was definitely giving her a look that meant she was late according to his tummy clock.

Instead of greeting her, he made a U-turn and padded off to the kitchen. There was no time to waste.

Maggie gave Snickers some canned food, shaped a new loaf of sourdough, and sat to eat her meal.

She couldn't get James's great-grandmother out of her thoughts—a new baby, no money, and her husband possibly going to prison. And now, to discover that his friend Sam could be descended from the man who had a part in ruining James's ancestor . . . it was a lot to take in.

If only I could find the second page of that letter.

Maggie took a bite of her salad and turned the questions over in her mind. Where was the rest of that letter? Would someone have hidden one page, but tossed the other? It didn't make sense.

There was something about the vellum paper that haunted her. *But what?*

When she finished eating, she slid the bread into the oven and set the timer. While she waited for the sourdough to bake, she went to her sitting room and worked on her sampler, a colorful calendar with a motif for each month. She needed a distraction from the letter.

But the thought of revealing what she knew made her heart ache. Everybody loved Sam Skyler. This discovery wouldn't go over well with her new friends.

It was starting to look like her findings were going to make her an outcast in her new town.

. . . .

Friday was crisp with a cerulean sky and cottony clouds. A quick check of her mailbox revealed a note from Nate. His daughter was home for the holiday, but his family would stop by for a few minutes on Thanksgiving. *Hooray!*

Feeling energized, she headed out to The Quilt Cupboard to replenish her embroidery supplies.

Fran was helping a customer coordinate swatches for a baby quilt. Maggie admired the young business owner. She had followed her passion for fabrics and stitching, and had made a successful career of it.

After the other customer left, Maggie carried several skeins of embroidery floss to the checkout.

Fran reached over the counter for a quick hug. "I was going to call you today. I want you to see what I've done so far. If you think the reweave shows too much, you can look around for a similar fabric to substitute. I don't have anything identical, but . . . wait here." She disappeared into the back and returned with Maggie's quilt. "It's your decision."

Accepting the magnifying glass Fran offered, Maggie leaned forward and inspected the tear, half of which had been rewoven. "I am astonished. It's beautiful. Such intricate work."

"Then I should keep at it?" Fran asked.

"Please do. It's wonderful." As Maggie handed back the magnifying glass, she realized she hadn't gotten an RSVP from Fran yet. "Can you make it to the manor on Thanksgiving?"

"I've got standing plans, but I'll try and stop by," Fran said. "I haven't been there since Evelyn . . ." She swallowed hard, her eyes glistening.

Maggie put her hand over Fran's. She knew her Aunt Evelyn had taken Fran under her wing and helped her open the quilt shop after she moved to town.

"She was a dear friend. Did I ever tell you how much she did for me?" Fran asked.

"Yes, but tell me again." Stories of her aunt's kindness were something she never tired of hearing. She was grateful that Evelyn's generosity didn't spring from a guilty conscience, something that might not be true of other families in town.

Some stories are best left untold. Had Aunt Evelyn thought the truth would do more harm than good?

"Fran, do you know Sam Skyler, the guy that's running for district attorney?"

"Sure. He's a good guy. I've always been surprised that someone as smart and promising stayed in a small town like this." She shrugged. "But he inherited all the wealth he needs, so I guess he just loves to serve."

Maggie was about to point out that someone as talented as Fran *moved* to this small town, but another customer came in, and Fran excused herself to help the newcomer.

With a wave, Maggie left her to her work.

Everyone she had talked to had nothing but praise for Sam Skyler. Maybe he was such a dedicated civil servant to make up for how his family made its fortune. But that didn't excuse breaking into her home and leaving threatening notes.

Maggie's next stop of the day was the Carriage House. She wanted to solidify plans with June for hitting a few last-minute sales that would really fill the shop before Black Friday. She entered to find her friend moving things around to fill in for some big-ticket items she had sold that morning.

"What time should we start the hunt tomorrow?" Maggie grunted as she helped move a black walnut rolltop desk.

"No later than seven. We have three indoor tag sales I want to hit, and the auction house is open early for viewing. I like to see what I'm bidding on. You can't trust photos." She pointed to the child-size Windsor rocker in the nursery vignette. "I thought that was for an adult when I bought it sight unseen."

Maggie laughed. "It's still a great piece."

"But even at break-even pricing, it's not a good deal." June smirked at the rocking chair as if it had affronted her.

"I'd like to bid on something." Maggie rubbed her hands together. "Aunt Evelyn always made it sound so exciting."

"That it is. But I don't bother with it anymore. I inspect the items and then leave bids with the office. They appoint a surrogate bidder and call us with the results. Then I send our payment back with the movers."

"That's kind of disappointing. I was looking forward to the thrill of the competition."

"Once a month they have a night auction for the high-end items. That's a lot of fun." June put a bronze piano lamp on the desk. "But you have to set limits beforehand. You get caught up in bidding and the next thing you know, you've ruined your profit margin."

She could see how that might happen. "So, if we leave at seven tomorrow, will we be done in time for you to open the shop?"

"No. I'll have to open late, but I doubt we'll lose any business in those couple of hours. The majority of Saturday traffic is tourists and tire-kickers."

Maggie lifted a brow. "Tire-kickers?"

"Browsers with no intention of buying."

Maggie made a mental note of everything June told her about running the business. Not that she wanted to replace her best and only employee—June did excellent work—but it would be foolish of Maggie not to know how to run her own shop. Plus, she loved antiques. She intended to learn everything she could about them.

· · · · · · · · · · · · · · · · ·

On Friday evening, as Maggie picked out her clothes for the next day, the questions that had been churning in her mind all day had solidified into leads she needed to follow. She sat and made a new list:

> *Find out if Sally Allen's father had been a vaudeville musician.*

> *Did Sally Allen's father ever return home?*

> *Were Sam Skyler's people Schulers?*

> *If so, when did the Skylers anglicize their name?*

It might upset James to think that she suspected his friend, and she had no idea how to tell him. She decided she would try in an email. She went to the office where she'd left her laptop and composed a note explaining what she knew.

But she couldn't hit the Send button.

Instead, she did a search for Sam Skyler. When she found his head shot on the county's website, she had to admit he looked friendly enough. But that didn't mean anything. It wasn't as if he'd have a tattoo across his forehead warning people to beware of him.

She scooped up Snickers and paced from the office to the library, where she stopped and stood in front of Captain Sedgwick. He reminded her with his steely gaze to be brave.

She gritted her teeth and marched back into the office.

Hoping James wouldn't hate her, she sent the email.

17

Maggie woke at five thirty to be sure that she had enough time to accomplish her morning activities before she picked up June. After she fortified herself with coffee and an egg sandwich, she checked her email to find a reply from James:

> *Maybe you should stop your research. I'm worried about damaging Sam's reputation and the town's chance at getting a great district attorney. We don't know how people will react if it turns out that his family wealth came from a bank robbery. He's a friend and a good person. I don't want to see him harmed.*

Maggie bit her lower lip. Had it not occurred to James that his friend could have broken into her house? He so staunchly believed in Sam that she doubted she could convince him of the possibility.

She rubbed Snickers's ear. "I'll be back this afternoon."

At their first sale—in a two-car garage in a residential area up the coast—Maggie purchased an Erté-style lamp and June found a mantel clock that could easily be refurbished. As she was haggling over the price, Maggie headed out to the Jetta. But she found her way blocked by a stocky bald man.

"How much?" he asked in a gruff voice, pointing to the lamp.

Maggie clutched it more tightly. "I paid three dollars."

"I'll give you five," he said, reaching for it.

"No thank you." She shifted it to her other arm, sidestepped him, and got into the car to warm it up and wait for June.

That was weird.

At the next sale, about a mile away in a fire station, the street was lined with cars, and Maggie parked around the corner.

She rummaged through a display of costume jewelry, looking for a mourning pin. They were more valuable if the photo of the deceased was still in them.

"No luck," she told June, who approached with a silver candlestick in each hand.

When they returned to the car, Maggie noticed the stocky bald man near it. He hastily retreated to his SUV—gray with a dented grill—and pulled away.

She got an uneasy feeling.

At the third sale, in a church basement, June scored an adult-size Windsor rocking chair in need of a new coat of stain. "This is exactly what I needed. If I pair it with the child's rocker, it'll sell as a set in no time." Elated, June got on her cell phone and made arrangements for her husband to pick it up in their SUV.

Maggie found a pair of brass marine lanterns with green and red glass that she would put in the nautical vignette. As she paid, the stocky bald man stood nearby, going through a box of baby clothes. She noticed that he was sweaty and he kept glancing up at her.

Her nerves were wearing thin by the time they reached the auction house. Maggie stuck close to June, offering vague opinions while barely looking at the pieces on offer. The stocky man had parked next to her Jetta, and she was preoccupied with keeping an eye on him.

When they left the auction house and the man got into his vehicle at the same time, Maggie snapped. "It's that same guy. I've seen him at every single sale, and now he's here, leaving when we are. I think he's been following us."

"Is that what's wrong?" June laughed. "I run into the same faces all the time. He's probably just another antique junkie."

Maggie wasn't so sure. He gave her a creepy feeling, and she noticed that he hadn't purchased anything.

Keeping an eye on her rearview mirror during the return trip, she was certain the same SUV with the dented grill was following them.

"Is your seat belt secure?" Maggie had meant to speak calmly so as not to frighten her friend, but she was clearly stressed.

"It's on," June said, a question in her voice.

"That gray SUV has been everywhere we have, and now it's behind us again." She gave a tug on her own seat belt.

June visibly relaxed. "It's the most common color of all the models. Mine's gray. At least three have passed us since we started the return trip."

"This one has a distinct dent on the grill." Maggie reduced her speed to ten miles per hour below the limit. "He's slowing down too. Any weekender worth his salt would go around us. He's definitely following us."

June turned to look, but didn't comment.

When Maggie returned to the speed limit, so did the driver. "Can you get his license plate number? There's a pad in my purse."

"No problem." June retrieved the notepad. "But it's not unusual to see familiar faces throughout the day. He could just as easily think we were stalking him."

But Maggie had no doubt that something was wrong, especially when she made a sudden turn and the SUV followed her around the corner, tires squealing.

Accelerating to get some distance ahead was fruitless. The SUV stayed on her tail.

June gripped the sides of her seat.

This is probably a bad plan, Maggie scolded herself. She should have driven straight to the nearest police department or a public place, not a secluded back road.

"Hang on!" The words were barely out of her mouth when the SUV hit the bumper of the Jetta with a bang.

June let out a yelp.

They fishtailed toward the pine trees on the side of the rural road, but Maggie steered into it and got the car under control.

The SUV hit them again, but she accelerated right before the impact, allowing her to maintain control of the car. She was going way too fast, but so was the SUV driver on her tail.

She squealed around a corner, reasoning that her little car would be able to turn faster than the top-heavy SUV. They raced through a small neighborhood, her Jetta pulling ahead with every turn.

Finally, civilization was in sight. Maggie careened back out onto the main road as a few drivers honked at her. She was betting the SUV driver wouldn't try anything with witnesses around. But just in case, she passed a few cars to try to put some distance between the Jetta and its attacker.

Maggie managed a glance at June, who was pale and wide-eyed. "Are you okay?"

"I think that man is following us," June deadpanned.

Maggie might have laughed if she hadn't noticed the SUV weaving through traffic to catch up with them. "Would you dial 911?" They were close enough to the town of Seacliff that their call would go through.

June dialed and gave them the information. She placed her hand over the bottom of her phone. "The dispatcher wants me to keep the line open. A marked car is on its way."

After a few minutes, a patrol car passed them going in the opposite direction. Before it got the opportunity to do a U-turn, the gray SUV turned off the main drive and disappeared.

"He's getting away!" Maggie exclaimed. "Tell them he turned when he saw the police car."

June told the dispatcher and then relayed instructions to Maggie. "The operator said we're to follow the police escort."

"But he's getting away!"

"I guess it's more important to keep us safe." June settled back into her seat.

At the station, after she reported the hit-and-run, the police officer scolded Maggie. "We got a few calls about *your* reckless driving."

"We were being attacked!"

The officer shook his head at her but dropped it. "We've got the plate number. We'll keep an eye out."

Maggie felt like they'd gotten the brush-off.

On the way back to Somerset Harbor, June said, "I guess we know why that SUV has a dented grill, eh?" It was clear she was trying to break the tension.

"He probably wasn't after us at all," Maggie joined in. "He's just a terrible driver."

June demurred. "No, he's a good driver. He's so good, he can drive while he's drinking his coffee, changing the radio station, and talking on the phone."

In the time it took to get to the Carriage House parking lot, they'd had a good laugh.

"Are you sure you want to open today?" Maggie asked.

June eased Maggie's hands off the wheel and held them in hers. "We're okay."

Maggie smiled and nodded. "How about I take our treasures to the manor to clean them up?"

June agreed, gave her friend's hands another squeeze, and hurried to open the shop for the weekend browsers who had pulled into the lot.

Not ready to be alone, Maggie decided to stop by The Busy Bean for lunch and a sympathetic ear.

She greeted Daisy and sniffed the air. "It smells like fall in here."

"I'm trying a new blend with dried apples, maple, and cinnamon. Will you be my first taste tester?"

"Haven't you tried it yet?"

"I may have to drink it all if nobody likes it. I'm saving room."

"Why not? I'm having an adventurous day. And I'll get a club sandwich to go with it."

"Coming up. Coffee, club sandwich, and a curious Southerner." Daisy hollered the food order to Jack in the kitchen and then poured the new coffee blend, a mug for each. "Tell me about your adventure."

Maggie gave an abridged version of the break-in, the notes, the stalker, and the high-speed chase. "He may be the same guy who tried to break into my safe."

"Well, I'm only a catfish-loving girl in lobster land, but if he was looking for something in your house, wouldn't he be there instead of following you all over the coast?" Daisy asked.

"You make a good point." Maggie gave it some thought as Daisy went back to the kitchen. Maybe the incidents weren't related. If that was the case, she was having a pretty bad string of luck.

Daisy returned with a huge club sandwich. "Those are homemade sweet potato chips. I'm trying to serve healthier."

As Maggie was trying one, the door burst open with a clatter. A bearded man rushed in. "Anyone here own a white Jetta? Someone's trying to break into it."

"I do!" Maggie jumped up, grabbed her cell phone from her purse, and dialed 911 as she hurried outside.

She and the bearded man ran toward the would-be carjacker, a stocky bald man who was taking a crowbar to her trunk. As they got closer, he saw them, leaped into his gray SUV, and pulled away with a squeal of tires before Maggie could complete the call to 911.

She reported the incident and told the dispatcher she would be in The Busy Bean. Then she extended her hand to the bearded man. "Maggie Watson. Thank you so much."

"Harry Carter, ma'am." He shook her hand, then held open the door to The Busy Bean.

"You're Daisy's husband." Maggie would have recognized him more quickly had she not been so upset. His golden brown eyes, dark brown hair, and short beard looked close enough to the family photos on the café wall. He was heavyset, although it was clear that his physique was from hauling lobster traps rather than eating too many of his wife's pies.

Daisy leaned over the counter to Harry with outstretched arms. "My hero. He's been working with lobsters so long that he's become like them—a hard shell outside but a real sweet softy inside."

"Cut that out, Daisy. You know that's a secret." Harry kissed his wife's forehead and sat at the counter.

After they had filled in Harry on what had been happening, the bell over the door rang and Officer Linton stepped inside. He nodded to the Carters before turning to Maggie. "You called, Ms. Watson?"

Maggie shook her head in frustration. "I don't know who that guy is, but I have his license plate number." She tore the page from her notepad and handed it to Officer Linton.

"Not many think that clearly under pressure." He took the paper and copied down the number in his own notepad.

"I didn't. That same gray SUV was following me up and down the coastline today while June and I were antiquing. She wrote down the plate number then. I called the police in Seacliff after he rammed into the back of my car."

"Was he tailgating?" Officer Linton asked.

"No, he was chasing us on a back road. I only got away because my car corners faster than his old dented SUV."

Officer Linton paused to consider the idea of Maggie leading a high-speed chase. Maggie could have sworn he looked mildly impressed.

"Do you have any idea why he was chasing you?"

"No," she said simply.

"You've had break-ins, prowlers, notes, and now this." Officer Linton spoke as he continued writing. "I'd say someone's interested in something you have."

"He'd have to tell you. I don't have any expensive items in the car."

"The license plate and car description are good enough to bring in the owner. But the owner may not have been the one driving."

"The driver is stocky, has a shaved head, and is wearing a plaid shirt," Maggie told him.

"He was wearing sneakers," Harry said. "And he's got bushy eyebrows."

Officer Linton added the description and then stuck his notepad inside his jacket. "I'll run the plates and bring him in for questioning. And I'm going to put you on the drive-by list. It might be wise to lock your car in the garage until we can arrest him. He may want something in there that you acquired today. Can you think what that would be?"

Maggie shook her head. "There's nothing of value in my car. He tried to buy a three-dollar lamp from me at a tag sale, but that's hardly worth prison time."

"However little you think you have, there's always someone who wants it." Officer Linton touched the bill of his cap. "We'll notify you when we have him in custody. For now, it's best to unload whatever you purchased today and keep your vehicle out of sight."

When Officer Linton left, Maggie slumped onto a counter stool. The lamp the man had tried to buy from her was lovely, but if he wanted it so badly, he could have increased his offer. The risks he took weren't for a cheap lamp. If he was the same person who broke into the manor, he was using it as an excuse to get at the letter. *To get at me.*

Maggie shuddered. *How far would he have gone?*

She mentally went over the list of local ephemera collectors again—Rutledge, Peters, Davidson, Wallis, and Skyler. She knew the man wasn't Davidson or Skyler. Neither was bald and stocky. *Rutledge, Peters, Wallis.*

If it had been any of them, June would have recognized him. She was back to considering that the events of the day were completely unrelated.

"They'll find him." Daisy patted Maggie's hand. "Now eat something. You need it."

But she had lost her appetite, so Daisy packed her sandwich to go.

After some weak protesting, Maggie let Harry follow her home in his truck. She parked the Jetta in the garage, and he helped carry the day's small purchases inside.

"Do you want me to check that everything's secure?" Harry was putting the antiques on the kitchen table while eyeing the windows.

"That won't be necessary." Maggie thanked him and sent him on his way, but then she went through the whole house and checked all of the locks herself.

"Why are we the ones locked away?" She looked down at Snickers.

He meowed sharply.

"I agree. It's not fair."

As she booted up her laptop in the kitchen, she phoned June. "There was another incident after I dropped you off. I went to The Bean for lunch, and the man in the gray SUV tried to break into my car, but Harry chased him away."

Her friend gasped. "It's a good thing you were there. Who knows what might have happened if you hadn't been in a public place."

A chill ran up Maggie's spine. "Officer Linton might want to talk to you about the stalker."

"No problem—shaved head, bushy eyebrows, stocky, terrible driver. I can describe him."

"You didn't recognize him, did you?"

"I've never seen him before. What do you think he was after?"

"I don't have a clue. Officer Linton suggested I keep my car in the garage until they arrest the guy. So even if you don't see it, I may still be home."

"Locked up tight, I hope." June's concern was clear in her voice.

"You too." Then Maggie assured June that the police were handling it, but deep down she wasn't so sure.

After Maggie settled down a bit, she checked her email. A note from the auction house notified her that she and June had won several of their bids, all for less than they thought they'd pay. The news was anticlimactic after the day she'd had.

She closed her laptop and turned her attention to the small items they had purchased at the sales. She inspected the art deco lamp that the stalker had offered to buy for five dollars. The metal figure was reminiscent of Erté, but it was obviously a reproduction, hardly worth much.

She touched the figure, and it wobbled slightly. Maggie retrieved glue from the junk drawer. A little dab would fix that right up. She unscrewed the figure, and when she lifted it away from the bolt, she saw a scrap of paper lodged inside.

Maggie pulled it out and unfolded it. Handwritten in pencil were numbers that looked vaguely familiar. She read them again, and a cold wash of fear bathed her.

She knew those numbers!

It was a combination to a safe.

My safe!

18

The small piece of paper shook in Maggie's trembling hand. For such a small cluster of numbers, it spoke volumes about what was going on at Sedgwick Manor. The man with the dented SUV *was* after the lamp. He knew it contained the combination to her safe.

But how could he possibly know that? Was he the one who broke into my home?

Until now she'd only had two suspects. She was ashamed to have even considered that James would do such a thing. And Sam Skyler was above reproach according to everyone in town, but he had motive and opportunity. At least now she had an alternative, but she didn't have a clue what the stocky man's motive was.

How did someone get the combination to my safe? And why is it in this lamp?

The whole thing felt surreal. Maggie dialed Officer Linton's direct number.

"Ms. Watson, we still haven't located the perpetrator, but does the name Mike Symms mean anything to you?"

"No, but I think I know why he was following me and what he was after. You've got to see it to believe it."

"We're out on routine patrol and not far away. We'll be at your front door in five minutes."

As she paced the long hall, it seemed five minutes had never taken so long.

She relaxed when she heard a car in the driveway but peeked out the window to be sure it wasn't the gray SUV.

Officer Linton and his sometimes-partner, Officer Janeen Crosby, stepped inside the manor.

Maggie held out the paper, her hand still shaking a bit. She explained how she had found it in the lamp.

"It appears to be a combination to open a lock." Officer Linton gave the paper to Officer Crosby.

"Not just any lock—the lock to *my* safe." Maggie tried to keep her voice even. "My personal safe. How would a complete stranger get the combination to my safe? I don't even remember it by heart. I keep it in my notepad, which is always in my possession."

"Yes ma'am. I understand." Officer Crosby flipped open her notebook and started writing.

"What am I supposed to do now?"

"You don't need to do anything," Officer Linton assured her. "We can handle this."

Officer Crosby touched Maggie's arm reassuringly. "We're going to see that nothing happens to you, Ms. Watson. We can arrange for protection and move you to someplace where you'll be safe."

Maggie folded her arms over her chest. "No, this is my home. I won't let someone drive me from it."

Officer Linton's cell phone rang, and he excused himself to take the call while Officer Crosby asked Maggie about security at the manor. She showed Officer Crosby the new locks and took out her own notepad where she'd written down the number of the cleaning service to whom she'd given a key.

Officer Linton rejoined them. "We're going to have a uniform stationed out here for now. There's been a new wrinkle."

Maggie didn't like the sound of that.

"Do you remember the address where you obtained the lamp?"

"It was our first stop." She flipped the page of her notepad and tapped the address with her finger. "What's going on?"

"A woman at that address reported her husband missing, a

Mike Symms. That's the same name the gray SUV is registered to. We pulled his photo from the DMV, and it fits the description you gave. We believe he's on the run. He's got a long history of petty theft, but nothing so sophisticated as to have the combination to a safe, unless . . ."

Maggie froze. "Unless?"

"Are there valuables in the safe that he might be aware of, Ms. Watson?" Officer Crosby asked.

"Insurance policies, deeds, my will, that sort of thing." *And the letter.* She was not about to drag innocent people into this mess and explain the intricacies of her research or the significance of the letter to important citizens of Somerset Harbor. Withholding that one little piece of the puzzle would not keep them from finding Symms anyway.

It was decided that Officer Crosby would remain on the premises until the assigned uniformed officer could replace her. "Maintain your routine, Ms. Watson, and try to pretend we're not here."

After Officer Linton left and Officer Crosby went outside to patrol the grounds, Maggie went into the kitchen to fix her bodyguard some cocoa and consider the new information she possessed. *Mike Symms must have owned the lamp. No wonder he was so intent on getting it back.* As she poured the cocoa into a thermos, her phone rang.

"I was heading home when I saw a patrol car at your place," James said. "Are you all right?"

"I'm fine. I'll tell you about it tomorrow. Are we still on for church?"

After they confirmed their plans and hung up, she wondered how much she should tell James about her latest adventure. Maybe by the time she saw him, the police would have Mike Symms in custody.

At least I hope so.

After eating her club sandwich for dinner, Maggie got ready for bed and slid under the covers. She shivered as she waited for them to insulate her from the cool room. Unfortunately, they could do nothing to insulate her from her problems. She'd brought her questions to bed with her, and they blocked her sleep.

Who is this man, and why is he trying to break into my safe? What does he have to do with the letter? The names Rutledge, Peters, and Wallis came to mind, but she had no way of connecting any of them to any of this mess.

Officer Linton had mentioned that Mike Symms had a history of petty crimes. Now she wondered if Sam Skyler had hired him to steal a letter that could make him and his family look bad. She'd have no clue how to hire a criminal, but Skyler would. His job brought him in daily contact with criminals, from major crimes right down to petty theft. He could make a deal—probation or a shorter sentence—in exchange for a little favor like stealing a document. He might even arrange for the paperwork to vanish, and it would be as if the perpetrator had never been arrested.

Snickers snuggled closer, purring contentedly, and his little serenade finally lulled her into a restless sleep.

. . . .

Maggie woke Sunday morning determined to be optimistic. The hint of sun through gauzy clouds was like a promise of a better day. She fed Snickers and laid out her church clothes, but she remained in her bathrobe and fuzzy slippers until she'd finished a second cup of coffee. If it weren't for the uniformed officer strolling the perimeter, it could pass for a normal day.

Maggie dressed in her favorite fall outfit, a chocolate-brown knit turtleneck, a tan plaid skirt, and brown boots. She finished the look with a silver necklace of engraved flat beads that Richard had gotten for her when they were on a dig in New Mexico after she found out that she was expecting Emily. The piece of jewelry still had the power to make her happy.

James arrived at the appointed time. "You made it sound like nothing last night," he scolded as she slid into the passenger seat. "There's a uniformed officer patrolling your grounds. What's going on?"

"I don't know how to shorten the story, so why don't I tell you the whole thing after church? I'll take you to lunch at The Lobster Quadrille."

James's expression wasn't that of a patient man. As they walked from the parking lot to the church, he pressed her again for a morsel of information, but she reassured him that all was well. She flashed him her most convincing smile.

"You're a terrible liar," James said.

In the vestibule, he guided her toward a nicely dressed couple, then shook hands with the man and lightly embraced the woman.

"Meet Sam Skyler, Somerset Harbor's next district attorney, and his wife, Rachel Denman Skyler. Folks, this is Maggie Watson, the new owner of Sedgwick Manor."

Maggie felt adrenaline shoot through her body. She hoped her face hadn't flushed.

"Sure, Evelyn's niece," Sam said as they shook hands. "We admired her. I'm sorry for your loss."

"She juggled so many good works, and she was a big supporter of the town," Rachel added. "We miss her energy and influence."

"Are you all moved in?" Sam asked. "Getting used to that big place?"

As they chatted, Maggie noted that Sam was as tall as James and nearly as attractive, with a sprinkle of gray amid the slightly wavy brunet hair, enough to give the appearance of maturity and dependability necessary in a district attorney. He met her gaze squarely, and she wondered if it was his nature to show that he had nothing to hide or if he'd simply learned to act that way.

When talk turned to the bid for DA, Sam's energy level rose noticeably. "It'll be a tough race. Davidson is pouring lots of money into his campaign. He's already flooding the radio and television with ads. He has quite a war chest."

"Money from all the dregs of society, no doubt." James frowned. "A friend to the reprobates of the world."

"Without those reprobates, I'd be out of a job." Sam gave a hearty laugh.

"And those posters he's been putting up illegally." James scowled. "At the next city hall meeting, I'm proposing that we count them up and charge him a fee for each. They're ruining the ambiance here."

Rachel caught Maggie's attention and angled herself for a private conversation. "Let's leave the boys to their politics. They won't miss us."

Sam's wife was tall and slender, and she seemed comfortable with herself. Her dark hair was the latest casual style, but she had the air of a trendsetter more than a follower. She looked as if she came from old money but wasn't impressed by it. "We have a little group we call Harbor Hospitality for newcomers. I'm sorry that we haven't been to see you yet. How are you settling in?"

"It's been easier than I thought for the most part." *Excluding prowlers, car chases, and break-ins.*

Rachel glanced toward Sam as the organist began to play. "We'd like to visit, if you're up for it, to help you transition to life here on the coast. We can answer questions and share experiences we've had with businesses—perhaps save you from a few unreliable ones."

"How thoughtful. I'd love to have you and your group stop by. I suppose everyone is preparing for the holidays, but let's make it soon after the New Year." Maggie knew that people were curious about her and the manor. "Actually, I'm having an open house on Thanksgiving Day. I would love it if you and Sam stopped by. And tell your Harbor Hospitality friends too. I'd be happy to meet them."

"That would be lovely. We have plans, but we'll try to make it."

Had she actually invited her top suspect to her home? It was a knee-jerk reaction. She had started throwing blanket invitations out into the world. "Tell your friends" was her new strategy. If half of her "maybes" and a few wild cards showed up, she'd have a proper party.

The organ music became louder, and James led the way to the pew behind the Lintons. Maggie patted Ina's shoulder and greeted Nora. "Where's Robert?" she whispered.

"He had a call about some fugitive and left early this morning."

"I hope he gets his man." *And I hope it's Symms.*

Maggie needed answers, and Symms was the only one she knew of who could provide them. Besides, the patrol at her house was temporary. She wondered what would happen if they didn't find him. Would they leave her to fend for herself?

In the middle of the choir's final song, right before Pastor David was to begin his sermon, Robert Linton slipped into the pew next to his wife.

He glanced back at Maggie, who raised her eyebrow in an unspoken question.

The terse twitch of his head told her all she needed to know. The fugitive had eluded them.

She forced a slight smile as if to say "Better luck next time," but Maggie was disappointed and scared. *Will there be a next time?*

19

With a heavy heart, Maggie joined the congregation in song. She wondered how Snickers was doing—home alone, probably petrified by the uniformed officer trudging around the manor.

James leaned in, his lips close to her ear. "I saw the signaling between you and Robert. Is that part of what's going on?"

She nodded. It was not a conversation that she was looking forward to. She pondered how he would react when he found out that the letter from his family heirloom was causing so much concern. She dreaded telling him her suspicions about his friend. Plus, Maggie had to admit, Sam hardly struck her as the criminal type.

Still, Sam had the most to lose if that information got out. All she had to do was link him to Mike Symms. It felt like an insurmountable task, particularly since Symms had successfully avoided capture despite the police having his mug shot and the make and license plate number of his vehicle.

After church, James and Maggie waited for Robert to emerge from the building. "What happened? How did he get away?" Maggie's voice came out shakier than she'd expected.

"It was probably a false lead in the first place. But every state and local cop across the area is on the lookout and has the information. If he hadn't run, it would have been low priority. But since he's a fugitive, they're paying attention. It's only a matter of time."

James managed to wait until Robert had left before he turned to Maggie with his hands on his hips. "Okay, what's the deal? Tell me everything and start at the beginning."

"I'll fill you in over brunch."

James huffed but drove straight to the restaurant.

At The Lobster Quadrille, the hostess seated them near a window, and the waiter appeared as soon as they were settled. "Ahoy there. My name is Reed, and I'll be your waiter this afternoon. Our special today is blackened redfish with saffron rice and roasted peppers. I'll give you some time to decide."

Maggie was entertained by the menu cover which displayed four lobsters faced off in a square dance, the official quadrille. It reminded her of the illustration in *Alice's Adventures in Wonderland* and those blissful days of undisturbed reading in Aunt Evelyn's library. That felt so far away now.

After they ordered, James leveled a serious look her way. "Tell me everything. Why are there uniforms patrolling your property? They wouldn't assign a bodyguard unless you're in danger."

Maggie clasped her fingers and rested her wrists against the edge of the table. Clearing her throat, she took a sip of lemon water to give herself time to decide how to start. She told James about the high-speed chase, the attempted break-in of her Jetta, and the safe combination hidden inside the lamp. She didn't leave out anything, she didn't sugarcoat anything, and she didn't editorialize. He could draw his own conclusions.

James sat stone-faced. A barely visible tic at the corner of his mouth was the only sign that he was upset.

She shrugged, pretending that she was unperturbed. "I'm sure they'll arrest this Symms character anytime now. He can't hide forever."

"You can't stay at the manor alone." His expression was grim. "I'll call my mother. She'll want you to stay with her."

The conversation ceased when Reed brought them bread and small tossed salads. Maggie flipped the cloth cover from the bread basket and inhaled the smell of the warm individual loaves.

When Reed left, she shook her head vigorously. "That's sweet, but I refuse to be run out of my own home."

James forked a cube of tomato with more force than necessary. "You are an exasperating woman." He put his fork down and glowered. Then his expression softened, and he sighed. "I admire you for not backing down." He reached across the table and placed his hand over hers for a quick squeeze. "How can I help you? I feel the need to do something useful, if not particularly heroic."

"You can help me figure out why that letter is so important that someone is going to this much effort to get it. I've examined it every which way I can think of, and I keep coming back to this name Schuler."

James bobbed his head in agreement.

Maggie took a steadying breath. *Here goes nothing.* "Did you know that the Skyler family name was originally Schuler?"

James stiffened, and his expression darkened. "No, I didn't. But it doesn't matter. I know Sam Skyler—maybe better than anyone."

Maggie nodded, encouraging him to continue. She wanted to know exactly why James trusted Sam Skyler so much.

"In high school he was the best friend to me anyone could be." He grabbed a mini-loaf of bread and tore it into chunks as he spoke. "He knew that I felt like I didn't belong. But one of the things he told me was, 'Fake it till you make it,' and that's what I did. I wouldn't be who I am without Sam, and I can say for certain that he's not your man."

Not particularly convinced, Maggie gazed out at the ocean. A lone figure stood on the edge of the cliff and tossed pieces of bread into the air. The seagulls were diving and shrieking, competing for every morsel that they didn't have to fish for.

Reed cleared away the salad plates and set their entrees before them.

They ate in silence for a few minutes and then made forced small talk. Maggie hoped that she hadn't spoiled an otherwise delightful meal for the both of them.

But James had asked for the truth, and she'd been honest. Sam Skyler had a motive. Yet she couldn't ignore the image of that elegant couple she'd met. Sam had looked her directly in the eye with unabashed friendliness, and his wife had been so warm and genuine.

Finally, Maggie laid her fork on the rim of her platter. "I like Sam and Rachel. I'm exhausted from all of this mess, so forgive me if I was insensitive."

"I understand. You need answers," James said, always the gentleman.

"So, we can agree that this petty thief Symms has no reason to want that letter for himself. He has no connection to it as far as we know. If that's true, then he must have been hired by someone, right?"

"He could be after what he thinks might be in the safe. Jewels? Cash? Bearer bonds? Gold bullion?"

Maggie laughed and agreed it was possible. "I don't understand how the combination to the safe got in that lamp. He must have had a conniption when he saw that his wife had sold his lamp at a tag sale."

"I'm glad that you still have a sense of humor about it." James grinned. "It is pretty funny when you think about it. Talk about inept thieves. But how did he get the combination in the first place?"

"That's what I'd like to know. I didn't leave it lying around. It used to be Aunt Evelyn's, but even as generous as she was with house keys, I'm positive she wouldn't share the combination to her safe."

"I had a client once who lost the combination to his safe. He had to contact the manufacturer, give them the ID number, and answer a series of questions before they would release the numbers to him."

"Questions like his mother's maiden name and where he was born?"

"Yes." James nodded. "I advise people to make up fantasy answers. It's too easy to get common answers through public records online."

"Ruth mentioned the same thing, but really, how common is it?" Suddenly, a thought came to Maggie. "Remember after the break-in how I had smudges on my fingers from the back of my safe? I thought the thief was dirty, but he must have done a rubbing of the ID number!"

"Not so inept after all."

When they were finished with lunch and had settled into James's car, he suggested they drive up the coast a bit, but Maggie declined.

"I've got to put up the last of my Thanksgiving decorations."

"You sound pretty cheerful about that." James gave her a smile. "Has Emily changed her mind?"

"No. But I'm proud that she's taking her studies seriously. Plus, with a stalker on the loose, I'm glad she's tucked away safely at school."

James agreed, then said, "My mother and I would love to have you join us on Thursday if you're not feeling up to staying at the manor."

"Thanks, but I'm going through with the open house even if the only one who shows up is the officer on duty that day. Maybe it will snow and I can build a snowman to join us."

"I doubt we'll get more than a dusting until closer to Christmas. Nature likes to save it up for the big day."

Maggie breathed in the cool air as she stepped out of the car, and James walked her to her door. "It feels like snow to me."

"I don't know. Maybe Vermont snow is different from coastal Maine snow."

"If I'm right about this, coffee's on you."

He agreed with a chuckle and then offered to stay at the manor with Maggie for the afternoon to protect her.

She declined his kind offer. "I have plans to talk to Emily." Then she pointed at the officer when he came into view on the property. "Also, I've got a bodyguard."

After James left, she gave Snickers his tummy rub before she changed into jeans and a sweatshirt.

She placed scented pillar candles around the house and lit them to be sure they wouldn't overpower the space. The spicy aroma was the perfect backdrop for decorating.

Maggie was about to carry the remaining decorations into the dining room when the landline rang. *Why's Emily calling me on the house phone?* She answered without checking the caller ID. "Sweetheart, you're early."

There was muffled noise.

"Hello? Hello?"

She heard a distinct click and then silence.

Goose bumps formed on Maggie's arms and the back of her neck. The hair on her head bristled.

Was that Symms calling to see if she was home?

20

Maggie convinced herself that the call was a wrong number and there was nothing sinister about it.

Then the phone rang again.

When she answered, she heard breathing and then nothing. It happened several more times within the hour.

She nearly jumped out of her skin when her cell phone sounded. *Now he has my private number too?*

With frayed nerves, she snatched the ringing phone and shouted into it, "Stop calling me!"

"Uh, Mom?"

"Emily, sweetheart, I'm sorry. I thought . . . never mind. How are you?"

Her daughter hiccupped. She'd been crying. "I had to see it online. It's so humiliating."

"Do you have some water with you? Nine sips holding your breath, Emily. I can wait." Her mind went to a terrible place, imagining her daughter in peril. Maggie bit her lip, waiting to hear.

"What did I ever see in him?"

After more disjointed clues, the story came together. Emily had been dumped by her high school sweetheart, Brandon Evans.

"Didn't you tell me that you were going to break up with him?"

"Yes, but I was still trying to think how to do it without hurting his feelings." Emily sniffed. "He obviously wasn't as considerate. He posted a photo online of him with Kimberly Grant. It's disgusting."

Maggie imagined her daughter twisting a strand of her hair the way she did when she was upset, pining over a boy whose most enthusiastic conversations involved his car's newest accessory and his latest mention on the local sports page. Heartbreak was anything but logical.

She listened to Emily and added an occasional murmur to let her daughter know that there was a sympathetic ear on the other end. She knew this pain would pass and eventually be nothing but a footnote in her history. Emily might even have a fond memory or two of her young love, but that didn't make her current suffering any less painful.

Emily eventually sighed. "I'm okay now. Thanks for listening."

By the time they hung up, Maggie felt certain her daughter would be all right. She had some serious doubts about herself though.

She flagged down the patrolman and told him about the phone calls.

"You'll have to file a complaint before the phone company can install a tap on your line. But if the caller is using different pay phones or a burner phone, that will make finding him more difficult."

Maggie suspected as much. "He's already proving pretty hard to find." If he was calling to see whether she was home, maybe he was close by. That gave her hope—and a healthy dose of fear.

"Could it be someone else trying to call?" the officer asked.

"Maybe." She wasn't sure of anything anymore.

While the officer called it in, Maggie went back inside, wondering what to do. She could turn off the house phone and rely on her cell phone, which was what her friends and family mostly used anyway. But her landline would still ring on the caller's end, and he might think that she was gone.

Would he be fool enough to come to the manor with his description on a BOLO for every officer in the state? Thinking about it made her head ache. She needed to concentrate on something else.

Maggie settled herself in the office and turned to her notes. If Sally Allen was the baby alluded to in the letter, the trunk belonged to her father, a musician who played The Palace during its death throes.

She searched online for bank robberies in New York in 1930. The articles she found were lurid enough to sell newspapers, but they didn't have sufficient specific details to be of much help.

Then she found something. Her heart pounded as she read the article. It was an account of a robbery that mentioned two masked gunmen and an unknown driver who got away. She checked the date and then checked it again. Sure enough, it had taken place three days before the date on the letter. It looked like she had found the robbery the writer mentioned!

She was thrilled . . . and crestfallen.

So the story was probably true. She had suspected as much. In fact, the personal correspondence she had told her more than the newspaper article did.

Still, she printed it out and tucked it in her file. She imagined Ruth would be proud of her for connecting the dots.

As for the present-day crime, she still thought that Sam Skyler might be involved somehow. James was adamant that he wasn't, and his loyalty to Sam was understandable. However, Maggie didn't owe the assistant DA anything.

She wondered about that saying, "Fake it till you make it."

Is Sam Skyler faking it?

. . . .

The day before Thanksgiving, the sky was nearly covered with tight rows of round, puffy clouds that looked like a herd of sheep. The air smelled like snow, and the morning newscast confirmed it.

Maggie was having coffee and looking at her list of things left to do for her open house when Officer Linton called.

"We got Symms, Ms. Watson. They caught him this side of the Canadian border, so there won't be any extradition hearings to delay his return. State troopers are bringing him back now. We're recalling the patrolman, but you can rest assured that you're out of danger."

"Has he said anything?"

"Not so far. They'll put Symms through the booking process, but the court is closed until Monday, so he can't be arraigned until then. He's our guest. I don't believe he'll be offered bail, considering his record and the fact that he was fleeing."

Maggie had thought that she'd feel better when he was arrested, but she still didn't have a clue who'd hired him. Until they discovered who was behind it, she wasn't as confident as Officer Linton that she was out of danger. "Thank you for telling me. Have a good Thanksgiving, and please feel free to stop by tomorrow with your family if you'd like."

After the foot-patrol officer left, Maggie put out corn for the birds and deer—it was getting harder every day for them to forage—and then went over to the Carriage House workshop. She wanted to glue the last panel of fabric lining into the trunk so it could dry over Thanksgiving.

As she put away the tools, she glanced out the window to see the first light snowflakes coming down like flour through a sifter.

She walked into the showroom to see June putting out the last of the Christmas decorations.

"It's starting to snow," Maggie said. "Do you want to close up?"

"I have a decorator coming in an hour. After that, I believe I will. I've got to rest up for the onslaught on Friday. Also, I need to get a few things for the veggie tray I'm taking to Mom's. I'm sorry I'll miss your gathering."

"Well, I'm not sure if anyone will be coming. I got a lot of maybes, so a few people might drop by." She smiled but lowered her gaze. The holidays were always hard for a widow. *Now I'm an empty-nest widow in a new town.*

She left the glue to dry, bundled up, and trotted home as fast as she dared on the slippery path. The flakes were coming faster, and Maggie was in a hurry to get inside.

Then she stopped.

She reminded herself that life wasn't a race from one task to another. She tilted her head back and watched the snow zoom toward her. She breathed in the cold air. It was her first snowfall at Sedgwick Manor, and she intended to remember it.

Slipping in through the side door, Maggie sighed content-edly as the warmth of her kitchen engulfed her. She removed her outerwear and hung it on pegs near the door. With Symms locked away until Monday, she turned her thoughts to holiday baking. It wasn't Thanksgiving without it.

Fortunately, she had an industrial-size freezer where she could store leftovers from her feast. And the root cellar under the back porch would soon be the perfect temperature if she needed it. So, there was no excuse not to go all out.

The turkey was thawed in the refrigerator and would be ready to roast tomorrow. She reasoned that it would be good practice for her to make a holiday meal in her new kitchen without expectant, hungry guests waiting.

After a few hours of work, flour peppered the front of her apron, and the heat of the oven had her working in a T-shirt. She was pulling a pumpkin pie from the oven when James called to see if she was all right.

"Yes, thanks. Officer Linton said they have Symms in custody. He'll be arraigned on Monday when the court opens again."

"He isn't talking?"

"He has to go through the booking process before one of the detectives can question him. I am anxious to find out who hired him." Maggie realized it was a sensitive subject since she suspected Sam, so she picked a new topic. "I just took a pie from the oven. It seems right to bake when it snows."

"Speaking of what seems right, do you think it's about time to bring my mother in on what we know?"

"That's your decision. You know her best." She didn't want to influence his choice either way. "I'm going to transcribe my notes on what we have so far, if you want to wait until I do that."

He deferred to her suggestion, for which she was grateful. However, the fact was that she was less worried about Deborah than she was about James. She felt his mother was hardier than he thought.

In the toasty kitchen, Maggie set her bread dough out to rise. Then she made Emily's favorite casseroles and set them aside to cool. The smorgasbord of savory and sweet aromas lifted her spirits.

Finally, when she'd done as much as she had the energy to do, Maggie relaxed in the kitchen nook to check her list. Everything was ready but the cranberry sauce, which was simple enough and quick to make.

Satisfied, she flipped back to her notes on James's family. Maggie decided to check the 1940 census, hoping to find a nine-year-old Sally Allen. She brought her laptop into the kitchen and typed in what little she knew. Drusilla was listed as head of household, which confirmed that Sally's father wasn't around.

James was right; it was time to bring Deborah up to speed on what they knew. She might be able to shed some light on what had happened to her grandfather. Even if she didn't know a lot about him, she could probably conjure up a name.

As Maggie was transcribing her notes, Emily called.

"You would not believe what's happening over here," she said.

"What is it? Are you all right?"

"I'm okay for now, but the snow knocked out the transformers, and that shut down the generators, and the whole campus is dark. All the buildings. The library, the dorms, the dining hall. It's getting cold, and there won't be any food service. There are only ten of us left on campus, but—"

Maggie exhaled. "Oh, is that all?"

"*All?* Mom, we'll be frozen to death by tomorrow morning."

"Of course it's terrible. I meant, are there only ten of you?"

"Yeah. The staff suggested that we go to an emergency shelter or a hotel, and then most of them left. But Bill, one of the shuttle bus drivers, is still here. He said he'd take us anywhere we decided to go."

Anywhere? The wheels in Maggie's mind were spinning. "What are the roads like? Can you get out?"

"It's snowing, but Bill talked with the highway patrol. If we leave within the next hour or so, the roads will be passable."

"Let me talk to the bus driver. You're all coming here. There's plenty of room."

"Everyone? But Mom, what about food?"

"Not a problem." Maggie smiled broadly. "Now go spread the word and put Bill on the phone." She gave him directions to Sedgwick Manor. "Take as much time as you need to get yourself and those kids here safely." She hung up, feeling like she might burst with joy.

"Snickers, Emily's coming, and she is bringing company!" Maggie reached down and scooped the unsuspecting tabby to her as she danced across the floor. Snickers squirmed out of her arms and retreated. "Wise cat."

She didn't want Bill to miss the manor, so she rushed through the house, turning on lights. Then she lit fires to make it cozy and warm inside.

Maggie hummed as she transferred the casseroles from the

cooling racks to the refrigerator. She checked the freezer and found two hams she'd bought on sale, bacon, sausage, and some containers of butternut squash soup she'd made. She pulled that out since it was Emily's favorite. She had plenty of eggs and potatoes. She could make a breakfast casserole and pancakes. *Young people eat like piranhas.* Between the freezer and root cellar, they wouldn't have to gnaw on the furniture.

There was a knock at the door, and Maggie ran to open it, exclaiming, "I'm so glad you got here safely!"

"How did you know I was coming? I wanted to surprise you." Fran was standing on the stoop, snow on her knit hat, and a bundle in her arms. "I finished mending your quilt and wanted to make sure you'd have it for Thanksgiving."

"How sweet! Thank you." Maggie raced on to explain her exuberance. "Emily's coming home. I thought you were her."

"That's wonderful news."

"Come in and warm up." She stood back and held the door open wider.

"I would love to, but the roads are getting bad." Fran glanced inside. "It looks beautiful. Evelyn would be pleased to know you kept up her Thanksgiving traditions."

Maggie was touched, and she thanked her new friend . . . for more than the quilt. *What wonderful, thoughtful people I'm getting to know here.*

"Please stop by the shop when you get a chance and let me know if you're happy with it." Fran waved and headed back to her car.

Maggie carried her precious blanket into her bedroom and spread it on the bed. She couldn't even see where the rip had been.

It looked like this would be a magnificent Thanksgiving after all.

21

It seemed like forever to Maggie before the headlights of the campus shuttle bus pulled into the driveway of Sedgwick Manor. Ten college students, loaded down with bags and still wearing their overstuffed coats, wool scarves, gloves, and hats, spilled from the bus, laughing and chattering merrily. They bustled through the open door, all politely greeting their hostess.

Snickers had long since skittered away.

Emily was the last to enter. She dropped her bags and hugged Maggie. "Hi, Mom. We're starved."

"Everyone leave your backpacks here and go into the kitchen for butternut squash soup, grilled cheese sandwiches, and hot chocolate."

A short, broad-chested man with a tinge of gray in his sideburns remained on the stoop.

"Bill?" Maggie asked. "You're welcome to join us."

The bus driver touched the brim of his cap. "Thank you, ma'am, but I only live about five miles from here, so I'll be going while I can. They think the outage will be fixed by Saturday."

He handed her a list of names, and the two exchanged phone numbers.

"There are ten kids here. When I return, I'll expect at least a majority of them." He winked. "Good luck."

"You be careful out there. And happy Thanksgiving." The snow was coming down with a vengeance, and Maggie watched as Bill boarded the bus and drove out onto Shoreline Drive.

At the door to the kitchen, she leaned against the jamb and grinned at the activity. There were eight young women—she was making a conscious effort to stop thinking of Emily and her friends as girls—and two young men.

"Mom, where's Snickers?" Emily asked. "Doesn't he know I'm here?"

Maggie noticed that she didn't say "home." It would take time. *Home is where the mom is.*

"He's probably under my bed." She pointed the way. "I'd guess he's a little overwhelmed."

After Emily left to greet the cat, Maggie introduced herself and tried to associate names with faces. No problem with the boys. Jerry had hair like a strawberry. Thomas had ruddy cheeks like Thomas Jefferson. The seven girls were Gina, Sophie, Bella, Piper, Crystal, Joan, and Millie.

Maybe I should make them wear name tags.

"Jerry, Thomas, I have a bedroom upstairs that's normally used for storage, but it has a couple of folding cots if you're not claustrophobic. Or you can hunker down on the bedrolls by the fireplace in the dining room."

They decided to use the room to stash their bags but camp out in the dining room at bedtime.

The girls—*young women*—divided themselves up in the second-floor bedrooms. Soon the hall was empty of backpacks, and the manor fell silent.

Her thoughtful young guests had cleared everything away, so all she had to do was turn on the dishwasher.

Maggie found Emily curled up asleep on her bed, the newly mended quilt tucked up to her nose. Snickers was nestled against her daughter, and neither of them stirred as she got ready for bed and crawled in beside them.

· · · · · · · · · · · · · · · · · ·

Maggie was startled awake by her alarm at six in the morning.

Emily wasn't there. She must have awakened in the night and gone to one of the bedrooms. *Had Snickers followed her? Traitor.*

Wanting to get an early start on the big bird and prepare breakfast for her visitors, she hurried to get ready for the day. As she dressed, she smelled coffee.

Who made coffee?

In the kitchen, Emily and a couple of the girls were bustling about. The coffee urn was perking. Eggshells, at least a dozen of them, lay in the compost bin. Crystal, a dark-haired girl with a pixie cut, was whisking their contents in a mixing bowl. Joan, who Maggie remembered was the one with a light sprinkling of freckles across her nose, said, "I'm making some pancake batter. I saw that the griddle was out along with maple syrup, so I figured that was what you were planning."

A bit dazed, Maggie nodded, fished a clean mug from the dishwasher, and filled it with coffee from the urn. Then she put the clean dishes away amidst the bustle. When she was finished and found there wasn't anything left for her to do—*many hands make light work*—she perched on a kitchen chair to enjoy the show.

Emily opened a can of cat food and put it in Snickers's bowl. "I saw you had the chafing dishes out. I thought we could use them since we'll probably be eating in shifts."

"Are the guys sleeping in?" Maggie asked.

Emily gestured toward the window. "No, they've already built a couple of snowmen, and now they're having a snowball fight." As she spoke, a clump of snow hit the window and slid slowly down the glass.

Maggie laughed. "Didn't any of you sleep last night?"

"I slept like a rock," Crystal said. "Your beds are way better than the ones in the dorms."

"We're used to getting an early start." Joan flipped pancakes as she spoke. "It's good practice for our careers."

While the young women shared nursing school survival tactics and career tracks, Maggie finished her coffee and set the turkey near the sink to get closer to room temperature. Then she pulled containers of juice from the fridge.

"Here, let me get that." Emily took the jugs from her mother, placed them on the buffet table, and set out the juice glasses.

Maggie watched with bemusement, wondering why she had ever worried about her daughter. Emily and her friends were incredible. "Any of you who didn't call your parents last night, please do so this morning and give them my number in case. I'll be happy to talk to them if they're worried."

When everyone had eaten and the dishwasher was once again humming and sloshing, Maggie trussed the turkey and put it in the larger of the two ovens.

While she was contemplating what snacks to put out to feed her guests before the feast, June called. "The snowplows won't reach here until after one, so we're not leaving town. Is the invitation still open to join you? I can bring my pecan pie, three-bean salad, and veggie platter."

Maggie was delighted. "The more the merrier." She told June about the houseful of college students, aware of the absolute glee in her voice.

As she hung up, she saw Jerry and Thomas traipsing down the hall with their arms full of cordwood for the fireplaces. A few moments later, Jerry stuck his head into the kitchen. "Anything else we can do, Ms. Watson?"

Happy for such eager helpers, she sent the boys upstairs to get several folding tables and chairs from storage. It was looking like she was going to need them.

While they were arranging the tables, James called. "A tree limb fell on the power line, and we have no electricity at my mother's or my place. I hate to ask, but—"

"Please, by all means, come over. But I suddenly have ten college students plus June and her husband. Will Deborah be all right in a crowd?"

"Let me get back to you." After a few minutes, James called again. "I've convinced her that there'll be so much going on that no one will notice if she feels like tucking herself into a quiet corner. I'll bring my cranberry salad. I also have a turkey breast and dressing."

"That sounds delicious."

He cleared his throat. "I've been coaxing some family history out of my mother. I think you'll find it interesting."

Maggie hung up, smiling. It was turning out to be a glorious first Thanksgiving in her new home! Until James mentioned the family history, she hadn't once thought about the break-ins, the letter, or anything remotely sinister all day. That was a monumental achievement.

As the afternoon progressed, the manor swelled with friends who'd had to cancel their plans because of the weather—Ina, Ruth, Robert and his family, Fran, Nate, and Opal. Maggie even made some new friends when Daisy and Harry showed up with a couple of lobster fishermen, their wives, and the wharf master.

"Word got around, honey," Daisy told her. "And it wasn't from me. It seems the eccentric heiress of Sedgwick Manor invited the whole town." She directed Harry to add her pies to the groaning board, which caused a new feeding frenzy among the young adults.

Whenever the food began to run low, someone would bring more. The huge dining table was so full that Maggie removed the cornucopia centerpiece to make room. Laughter and conversation rang throughout her new home.

When Sam and Rachel Skyler arrived, the party was in full swing. Maggie stationed herself in the kitchen to keep an eye on the route to her safe, but the Skylers didn't even glance in that direction. She had to admit, Sam was exactly as James had described him. *Down-to-earth.*

By six at night, the turkey was a skeleton and every dish appeared to have been licked clean by Snickers, who had gotten over his nervousness and spent a good bit of time in one lap or another.

Bill the bus driver called to say that the pond near his home was frozen solid, and someone had set up a skate-rental stand. He offered to bus anyone who wanted to go. The young adults were all up for it, and the manor was significantly quieter in their absence.

The party wound down quickly after the college kids left. Gradually, Maggie's friends departed with hugs and empty dishes until only James and Deborah remained. They settled in the living room with hot cocoa and a warm fire.

"Mother, tell Maggie what you told me about your grand-mother Priscilla."

Deborah stared into the fireplace, a frown marring her porcelain face. Flames licked about the cordwood, occasionally hissing and popping. She turned her gaze to her son, and he nodded. "James told me about the letter. I'd like to see it, if I may."

Maggie hurried to retrieve it from the safe and handed it to Deborah.

She read silently, her eyes filling. *I count the days until my return to your loving arms and to welcome our child into this puzzling world.* She said the words softly before looking up. "Maybe my grandfather didn't desert my grandmother after all."

"Didn't Priscilla suspect that something dreadful must have happened?" Maggie asked.

"She died well before I was born, and neither my mother nor my aunt talked about it much." Deborah shook her head slowly. "In fact, Aunt Drusilla said my grandfather deserted my grandmother and that was why she died of a broken heart.

My mother, Sally, grew up believing it was her fault."

"How awful. That poor girl. No wonder it colored her adulthood."

"And mine. Ours." Deborah's eyes rested on James. "My mother briefly broke from Drusilla's influence to marry, but when my father was drowned, she simply withdrew. It became a way of life." Deborah closed her eyes and grew silent.

Maggie leaned toward her and grasped her hand. How sad that this lovely woman had been sheltered from the soul-healing empathy of friends, all because of one woman's bitter outlook on life. But she still couldn't understand how Priscilla could have thought her husband had abandoned her after that letter.

"Priscilla's husband intended to return. That letter shows that he loved her deeply and was excited about Sally."

Deborah handed the letter back. "But he didn't return. Adam was his name. Adam Allen."

"Adam?"

Aunt Evelyn did know!

Maggie remembered her aunt's note—*Adam?*—in the margin of the book about entertainers going to California for the movie industry.

"Something must have happened to him." Maggie didn't believe for a moment that he went to California. "We'll keep searching until we know what." She turned toward James. "Right?"

"Right." He leaned over and patted his mother's hand reassuringly. "It's possible that she never got the letter."

"As soon as the kids return to campus, we'll figure out what happened." Maggie felt certain she was up to the task now that Deborah was in the loop. "The answer must be somewhere. The truth needs to come out, even if only for your own peace of mind." She so badly wanted to free Deborah from whatever secret had imprisoned her.

Some stories are best left untold. But Maggie wasn't so sure of that. She had to admit that she never actually believed it.

In a cacophony of chatter, the students burst through the door. They poured into the room and merrily told overlapping stories about the outing. Then they disappeared into the kitchen when Deborah mentioned that she thought her whoopie pies were still in the fridge.

James rose and took his mother's hand, helping her to her feet.

Maggie hugged Deborah. "Thank you for sharing your story. I'm honored that you trust me with it. If I get any leads, I'll let you know. But I'm convinced that Adam Allen didn't abandon his family."

Deborah dabbed the corners of her eyes. "There was a lot of love in that letter."

"If only we could find the rest of it," James said.

Shortly after they left, Bill called. The college's power outage was fixed, and the campus would be back in business by the time he picked up the students at ten the next morning.

Maggie set out fixings for ham and cheese sandwiches, and then she and Emily paired off to catch up together for a bit. It was her favorite part of the day. After everyone ate, Maggie shooed them out of the kitchen and cleaned up. The noisy herd of young folks quieted as they turned the dining room into a makeshift study hall. Maggie retired to her bedroom, exhausted and content.

She was sure this had been the best Thanksgiving Sedgwick Manor had ever seen.

....

22

....

On Friday morning, Maggie stood in the doorway, her breath making fog in the chilly air as she waved goodbye. Those sweet kids had given Sedgwick Manor new life and chased all of the mysteries away for a time.

Snickers sat in the hallway, glaring at her accusingly.

"I'm sorry, kitty, but it is against the law for me to keep them."

Running laundry and putting things away, she wondering how things were going at the antiques shop. With all the snow, June had said she didn't expect the typical Black Friday onslaught. "Please call if things get crazy," Maggie had insisted. "I can be there in a jiff." Emily's thoughtful friends had shoveled the path to the antiques shop, so she wouldn't have to snowshoe there.

As she bustled around the house, putting it to rights, she couldn't keep her mind off one question: *How had Adam Allen simply disappeared without a trace?*

It wasn't possible for a person to vanish. There had to be some clue as to where he'd gone, whether it was people who remembered him from the band or people who had lived with him in the boardinghouse. They were all no doubt deceased by now, but perhaps there were diaries or letters that lived on.

Maybe no one ever found him because no one ever looked.

Maggie found it hard to believe that Priscilla hadn't inquired when Adam didn't return. She knew from the letter that Adam planned to report the crime. She imagined what it must have felt like to receive a trunk with all of his worldly possessions but no husband to go with them.

Why hadn't Adam gone home? Did he simply shed all remnants of his former life and take a new identity? It seemed unlikely.

He had written, *Schuler told me not to go to the police.* What if it wasn't a suggestion but a threat? Would Schuler—or Skyler, as he was later known—have committed murder to keep his secret?

As for Sam Skyler, having an unrepentant bank robber in his background could deflect from his message to the voters. But having a murderer in his family tree? The media would concentrate solely on that and ignore his accomplishments. Voters could be fickle. It was certainly true that elections were lost over more insignificant things.

While Maggie didn't know Sam Skyler very well, everyone in town seemed to respect him. James felt strongly that Sam was innocent, so she had to seriously entertain the idea.

If Skyler wasn't the culprit, who would have hired Symms?

After checking to see that June didn't need her help, Maggie visited the historical society. There she booted up the computer with its access to ancestral sites. She first checked the list of deaths in New York City in 1930, but she didn't find an Adam Allen. There were a good number of John Does, but with few clues other than their perceived ethnicity and approximate height and weight, that didn't help her.

She searched for news articles with the key words *bank robbery* and *Adam Allen*. She wanted to eliminate the possibility that Schuler or his companion had murdered the young father-to-be. She researched suicides and homicides, which included involuntary manslaughter and murder.

Maggie honed in on articles on and around the day Adam Allen wrote to Priscilla. She had almost given up when a story caught her eye: *Unidentified Male Killed by Trolley.*

Could that have been Adam Allen? Had fate delivered such a freakish and tragic blow? The article said that the victim had carried no wallet, but he had a playbill from The Palace Theatre in his coat pocket.

Maggie reread that line, her eyes wide. Had she actually found Adam Allen?

The story went on to say the accident happened right outside the Fifty-Fourth Precinct, so at least Maggie now had a year and location.

She called the New York City coroner's office. "What happens to unclaimed bodies?" she asked. "This would have been in 1930."

"After a year, their cremains are buried in the city-owned cemetery. The container is labeled, and we maintain a record of exactly where it's buried. Sometimes someone makes a claim years later, so we're prepared. But I don't think there's ever been a request as far back as yours," the assistant coroner told her.

Had Adam's cremains languished in a grave all these years with no more than a date and number while his family believed that he had abandoned them?

Maggie ran a hand through her hair, thinking. The Great Depression had been difficult, and otherwise-good people had done desperate things to survive. It was likely that someone snatched Adam's wallet before an officer could reach him.

She dialed James and relayed what she had discovered. "It's a long shot, but—"

"Wouldn't it be great if we could place his remains next to Priscilla and end the speculation once and for all?" he said. "By the way, my mother is remembering more. Talking about family history has opened the floodgates of her memory—of both of ours. Once, when Drusilla was in a good mood, she told my mother that Adam had the trunk made when his career was going well. Mother told me about another trunk—a small one—in the attic. It belonged to Drusilla. I thought you might like to be here when we open it."

"I'd be honored," Maggie said. "I have one more thing to chase down, and then I'm ready for a break, especially if it might be the key to the mystery. Incidentally, they'll have to let Symms loose on Monday if they haven't charged him by then."

"You shouldn't stay at Sedgwick Manor alone if he's released. It's too dangerous."

"Well, the day's not over. We may hear yet."

After Maggie hung up, she researched Schuler and Skyler in 1930 and 1931 in the online newspaper archives, but they were spotty at best. Before giving up entirely and going to the newspaper office to search their archives, she went through all of the filing cabinets to see if anything caught her eye. A thick folder marked *To Be Scanned* seemed promising. Inside were several newspaper clippings of local interest.

On an old, deteriorating clipping deep in the pile, she found the headline *Conquering Hero Comes Home*. The article was about how Isaac Schuler had left Somerset Harbor at the age of seventeen and returned before his twentieth birthday, a successful entrepreneur who invested his wealth in real estate. It mentioned that he had anglicized his surname upon return.

Behind that article were numerous clippings about the wealthy real estate developer who changed the coastline of Maine, leaving a fortune for his progeny. He paid off the debt for many houses in Somerset Harbor so families could stay in them without fear. The Allen home was included in that list.

Satisfied that her theories were confirmed, Maggie hurried to Deborah's to report what she had found. On her way, June called to report on how business was going at the antiques shop. "We've had so many sales! We'll need to go shopping again soon."

Maggie was elated at the news, mostly because June was so pleased. Her enthusiasm was infectious, and she felt hopeful as she made her way up the shoveled walkway to the Bennett home.

Deborah welcomed Maggie into the parlor. "James is bringing the trunk down now."

"Does he need help?"

Deborah smiled. "It's only a small hope chest."

Maggie wondered if anyone else noticed the symbolism in that. Considering what she knew of Drusilla's personality, there probably had been very little hope stored in that chest. Young girls at that time had embroidered linens, stitched items, and heirlooms, which were stored away along with dreams and wishes in preparation for marriage. It wasn't difficult to imagine that Drusilla had few.

Maggie could feel her body grow tense as James entered with the box, which was about the size of a sewing machine cover. *Will the secret behind the letter be revealed at last?*

Deborah looked relaxed, but Maggie felt as if she would burst with curiosity.

James set the box on the stool between her and his mother. The beautifully carved trunk was about half the size of a steamer trunk. She guessed it had been an heirloom in Drusilla's time. James opened it, allowing a whiff of stale air with a hint of cedar to escape.

There were two pairs of white-on-white embroidered pillowcases and a matching top sheet with a similar design. The chest also held kitchen towels in yellow and bath towels in white.

"I've never seen inside." Deborah fingered the fine embroidery work. "I remember my mother saying that no one had. When Drusilla died, my mother simply carried the trunk to the attic and pronounced herself free."

As Deborah handled one of the pillowcases, an envelope fluttered from it to the floor. Maggie picked it up.

"This fell out." She handed it to James, who pulled a folded piece of paper out of the envelope.

Dear Priscilla, he read aloud, *If you are reading this, forgive me for not telling you the truth of what happened to your husband. I let you think that Adam deserted you—you and little Sally—out of heartless jealousy. He met and wooed me first, you remember, but when he met you, it was as if I no longer existed. When his letter came, I read it and hid it from you. I still think I was right to hide it, since he never came back after all. I was only thinking of myself at the time, but I kept it hidden out of love for you. Forgive me. Drusilla.*

James put the letter down. "Priscilla died first. She never knew that Adam had written to her."

"What a terribly sad story." Maggie blotted tears from her eyes before they spilled onto her cheeks.

"I suppose Drusilla's guilt caused her to lash out at Sally. And then I had to find that trumpet in Adam's trunk. The way she came after me was frightening." James stared off for a moment, and the room was silent. "It disappeared the next day, and I thought I might disappear too."

Maggie's heart ached for him.

James held the paper to the light. "It's the same watermark as Adam's letter."

"We had a box of that stationery someone had given us," Deborah said. "Drusilla used it for everything—to wrap gifts, line drawers, protect tables from scratches."

James snapped his fingers. "Of course." He snatched up Deborah's hurricane lamp and ripped away the pad, then shrugged. "No such luck, I guess." Seeing the women's puzzled faces, he explained. "I thought maybe the rest of Adam's letter was hidden inside. Like the combination to Maggie's safe was hidden in the lamp she bought from that garage sale."

"Actually, there's a matching lamp in Emily's bedroom at the manor. And it's got vellum paper on the bottom."

"Let's go." James leaped up and made a beeline for his coat.

He stopped and added sheepishly, "If that's okay with you."

"Of course. I hate to get my hopes up, but I've got to know."

As Maggie drove home, the black Mercedes behind her, her pulse quickened. *Could we be lucky enough to find the missing page?* She couldn't get home fast enough.

She kept thinking about Drusilla's confession. Her jealousy had affected others through the generations. Maggie was amazed and saddened to see how it had rippled through time.

Inside, Snickers protested as they rushed past him and up the stairs to Emily's room. Maggie turned the lamp over and found the now-familiar stationery on the bottom. Carefully easing the paper away, she saw words in that same oxblood-color ink. She held it up so James could see.

The paper had been cut to fit the footed bottom, but key words were there: *54th precinct . . . shipped trunk . . . follow soon . . . love never ending . . . Adam.*

That was enough to tie it to the coroner's report. Adam Allen could come home at last.

"He must have been on his way to tell the police everything, but he was hit by the trolley before he could."

"Such a sad story," Maggie said quietly. *Almost as tragic as yours and Natalie's,* she thought. But no, it was better to let him broach that subject when he was ready. She would hold her peace until he did, if he ever did.

Downstairs, she dropped into an armchair in the library. It had been an emotional day.

"I'm glad to know the truth finally, but I'm not sure how it helps you." James sat on the settee. "I doubt that Symms has any personal interest in that letter. Surely he wouldn't risk jail for it unless he was paid handsomely. And I honestly can't see Sam doing anything illegal to keep a bad ancestor secret. He would resign his job and not run for district attorney if he thought that his past would interfere with the people's trust of him. And that would be a true tragedy for this town."

She nodded. "After meeting him, I have to agree that it seems unlikely. But then who hired Symms? What do they have to gain by having the letter?"

James rubbed his chin, staring into the fireplace.

Maggie sat up suddenly, an idea flickering at the corners of her mind. "What if the thief wanted to expose the letter so Sam would resign? Who would have the most to gain by that?"

"Davidson!" they exclaimed together.

"But how could he have known about it?" James wondered aloud.

"That's simple enough," Maggie replied. "June told him."

"June? Why on earth?"

"Davidson is an ephemera collector. She notified him about it before she knew I was keeping it a secret. Schuler dealt in real estate, and Davidson probably looked into the history of all the property in Somerset Harbor after becoming a landowner here. He must've put two and two together and figured out that the Schuler mentioned in the letter was Sam's great-grandfather."

"The only way Davidson could possibly beat Sam is to somehow paint him with the same brush as his ancestor and keep saying it until the voters would hear Sam's name and think felony." James clenched his fists.

"And from what I know of him, he would be able to find an ex-con eager to earn some money."

As they hashed out their new theory, the door knocker sounded. It was Officer Linton, and Maggie invited him in.

"I wanted you to know that Mike Symms is talking. He was hired by—"

"Jeff Davidson," Maggie said, finishing his sentence.

Robert's jaw dropped. "How did you know?"

"Long story."

"At any rate, Davidson's ambitions for district attorney are over," James said.

Officer Linton insisted on hearing the evidence, so Maggie ushered him into the library. As they were sitting, the door knocker clattered again.

Maggie opened the door, expecting to see Officer Crosby. "Why, hello! What a surprise."

"Am I late? The open house is today, isn't it, young lady?"

"James! Robert!" Maggie called out. "You'll never guess who's here." Turning to her guest, she smiled. "As a matter of fact, you're right on time, Mr. Davidson. Come on into the library. Do you know James Bennett and Officer Linton?"

She closed the door and followed Davidson into the library, treasuring the shocked look on his face when handcuffs were snapped onto his wrists and he was read his rights.

After the three men left, Maggie studied the portrait of the captain. The dim, flickering firelight seemed to bring a slight smile to his lips.

Hearing a melodic little meow at her feet, she picked up her cat and hugged him.

"Snickers, I do believe Captain Sedgwick approves of us after all."